TIDES OF FORTUNE

SHORT STORIES

Harold Raley

TotalRecall Publications, Inc.
1103 Middlecreek
Friendswood, Texas 77546
281-992-3131 281-482-5390 Fax
www.totalrecallpress.com

Copyright © 2021 by: Harold Raley
Cover Photo by: David Mark
Cover Design by: Bruce Moran
All rights reserved

ISBN: 978-1-64883-006-8
UPC: 6-43977-40068-0
Library of Congress Control Number: 2020939612

FIRST EDITION
1   2   3   4   5   6   7   8   9   10

Table of Contents

Authors Bio

Novelist and short story writer, linguist, philosopher, and professor, Harold C. Raley holds degrees (BA, MA, PhD) in English, Foreign Languages, Humanities, and Philosophy. Named Distinguished Professor, he has taught languages, literature, and philosophy in American and foreign universities. His publications include fourteen books of fiction, history, language, and philosophy, and approximately 150 articles and essays on wide-ranging topics in professional journals and newspapers.

Foreword

These are tales of fortune and forfeiture, happiness and hazard, love and deceit. Some stories are set in specific times and places but not confined to them. Others arise in the mere vastness of the world and belong anywhere applicable or nowhere definitive. For wherever there is human life, there are the yearnings, dreams, possibilities and impossibilities we call tales and stories. For this reason, I do not think of myself as their creator, but only their author or perhaps their channeler. I say this because the people who come to life in this book do not always behave as I wish and plan. I push and they push back. Which is why I am as surprised as the next person by what they decide to do and who they choose to be. Perhaps their way is best. For if the decisions were left up to me, most likely I would be their tyrant. As it is, I end up being their friend.

The Tattletale Letter

It seems that everything mysterious soon becomes mundane. Let me illustrate what I mean by retelling an account based on an incident I found tucked away in an old Spanish chronicle.

Because most Native Americans had no written language, they were mystified by the scratches on parchment to which early Spanish conquistadors and missionaries attached great importance. When they asked about the odd markings, the Spanish explained to the native people that they were words. This caused even greater confusion. How could they be words, the Native Americans reasoned, if they made no sound, yet could be heard by the Spaniards over great distances? The only words they knew were the ones they heard spoken, nothing they could see. Since these soundless words seemed illogical to their cultural way of thinking, in the beginning of their dealings with the Spanish, they looked on writing as a form of magic and regarded it with superstitious awe. To them it seemed that the marks on the parchments could hear and see in their silent, mysterious way and then tell others what they knew. At first, they could conceive of no way to get around these magical missives that seemed to know everything yet uttered not a word that a normal person could hear. But awed or not, the native people started to seek ways to outwit the conquerors' magic.

Finally, two runners thought they had hit on a workable tactic. It began when the Catholic Prior they served ordered them to deliver a letter and two strapped-on baskets of delicious fruit—apples, oranges, mangos, bananas, berries, and nuts—from their fertile Peruvian valley farms to the commandant of a Spanish fort in the Andes. The journey was long and the young runners, increasingly tempted by the succulent fruit they were carrying, lusted for a taste.

"If we eat the fruit, the letter will tell the commandant and we will be whipped," whispered one runner so the letter could not hear him.

For a long time, they jogged on in their tireless trot, ascending ever higher along the twisting mountain trail. Finally, one of them stopped, excited by an idea that might allow them to outsmart the all-knowing letter.

"If we hide the letter behind a tree or a rock while we eat without saying anything," he explained "it won't see or hear what we're doing and can't say anything to the Spaniards, can it?"

"Who knows, brother? I want a taste of the fruit as much as you do, but I fear their magic even more."

But eventually hunger wore down his reservations and the two hid the letter and silently but happily ate some of the fruit. But when they reached the fort, the commandant read the message, checked the baskets, and asked about the missing fruit. Naturally the frightened men at first denied any knowledge of it but finally had to confess they had eaten it. The commandant ordered his lieutenant to whip them. But before their punishment, one runner asked the commandant how he knew about the fruit.

"*Señor Comandante,* we hid the letter, so it couldn't see or hear us, so how could it know what we were doing?"

The amused commandant replied with a straight face, "Oh, but the letter knows anyway. Our letters always see and hear everything, so don't lie again. This time you get off with only a whipping. If you do it again, your punishment could be much more severe. And beware; the letters will be watching you."

The sore and chastened runners jogged back to the valley and spread the word to their kinsmen. The warning worked, but not for long. In time the Native Americans caught on and began to master the mystery of the written word themselves.

As I said, the mysterious soon becomes mundane.

The Gold Coins

Many stories have come down to us from ancient times of Hasan ibn Al-Rashad, at first Satrap and then Sultan of Damascus. He was famed throughout the caliphate and neighboring kingdoms for his astuteness in battle and his benevolence as the ruler of a vast empire. He was the terror of his enemies, who were no match for his tactics in battle, and revered by his subjects, who believed themselves favored of God for his firm but benign rule. He judged men by their character, not their religion. Though himself devoted to the teachings of the Prophet, of whom it was said—though not by him—that he was a descendant, at times he chastised the powerful imams themselves for their mistreatment of his subjects, including non-Muslims. For he dispensed evenhanded justice to Muslim, Jew, and Christian alike. The following story of the bag of gold coins illustrates why he was so highly esteemed.

*****

A poor streetsweeper appeared at the entrance to Sultan Hasan's magnificent palace and with considerable trepidation asked permission to plead his request for justice before the mighty ruler himself. At first dismissed because of his slovenly appearance and the Christian crucifix hung about his neck, he persisted and was finally admitted to the court of the great monarch. When it came his turn to speak his grievance, he declared that while cleaning away debris collected before the mosque he uncovered a bag of gold coins. And learning that a wealthy merchant had posted a handsome reward for the finder, he hurried to his establishment to collect it. The merchant received him, eagerly took the bag of coins, and hastened to his private quarters to verify its contents. Then he returned to the expectant sweeper. But instead of rewarding him for his honesty, the merchant berated him for thievery and demanded that he return the missing coins.

"But I took nothing from the bag, your grace. The bag and its contents are as I found them,"

"How many coins were in the bag when you uncovered it?"

"Thirty-five, by my count, your excellency, and I removed none."

"Liar! There were only thirty in the bag you returned to me! On my order my servants will now forcibly remove you from my property, and you may thank merciful Allah that I do not have you hauled before the magistrate and punished more severely for your crime!"

So saying, the merchant summoned his servants who beat and kicked the poor sweeper, leaving him bruised and bleeding in the cobblestone street. Thus, instead of being rewarded for his honesty, he was abused for his trust in the merchant's fairness.

Sultan Hasan listened attentively to the poor man's account, for not only did he dispense justice without regard to the rank and station of his subjects but acted in such matters as quickly as possible. For he could read the hearts and thoughts of men and was able to discern at once their honesty or deceit. Thereupon he sent a messenger to the merchant with orders that he present himself immediately at the court with the bag of coins.

Shortly thereafter the merchant arrived with the bag in hand, and Sultan Hasan asked him for details of the matter.

"By the Prophet, great sovereign, I am the victim of this man's chicanery. Some time ago I lost a bag of gold coins, earned in the lawful and honest transactions of my business. The man standing there in your august presence brought this bag to me in hopes of receiving the reward posted for the finder. But first he stole some of the coins. Five were missing. When this became known to me, I had him thrust out of my establishment, for I cannot abide dishonest men in my presence. Thus, it is evident, great lord, that instead of a reward for returning the bag, he deserves punishment for stealing the five missing coins."

The sweeper paled at the merchant's words. For who was he, a mere streetsweeper and Christian besides, in comparison to the wealthy merchant?

"Let us examine the matter carefully and with due deliberation, said the Sultan, for it seems that something is amiss in the details presented before us. To begin with, how many coins say you, esteemed merchant, were in the bag when you lost it?"

"Thirty-five, may it please you, great sovereign."

"And how many coins now remain by your count in the bag the sweeper delivered to you?"

"Only thirty, great lord."

"Let us now count the coins ourselves, lest there be some mistake. Bring the bag to us."

A servant hastened with the bag to the sultan, who then carefully counted the coins.

"It is as the merchant said: we count only thirty coins. Now let both merchant and sweeper again count the coins."

Once this task was completed, the sultan asked both men the number of coins in the bag.

"Thirty," said the merchant, sure that the Sultan was about to decide the case in his favor.

"Thirty," intoned the saddened sweeper, fearful that the great lord was about to rule against him.

"And do both men swear by what is most sacred to them that what they say is true and exact?"

"I so swear, supreme sovereign," said the merchant.

"I swear before you, great lord, that my words are true," declared the sweeper.

"Thirty then it is by all counts here rendered and sworn to us in this court, and verified by our own inspection," Sultan Hasan concluded. "Now then let us see the consequences of this number sworn and agreed to singly and severally.

"First: if this sweeper were a thief, he would have behaved like a thief by keeping all the coins and returning none. For the worth of the whole exceeds by far the sum of the offered reward. Second: it follows, therefore, that the bag presented at the court is not the one the merchant lost. For he has sworn that his bag contained thirty-five coins and that the bag found by the sweeper holds only thirty coins. We accept his account, for we cannot doubt the sworn word of an upstanding merchant, nor what we have seen with our own eyes. Third: since it is obvious that the sweeper is not a thief and the bag is not the one the merchant lost, our judgment is as follows: (1) the merchant shall continue to search for his missing bag of coins, thirty-five in number, and be ready to grant a fair reward to anyone who may chance to find his lost property. And (2) inasmuch as no rightful claimant has come forth to claim ownership of the thirty coins the sweeper found, they shall be his to keep. So we have ruled and so it is decreed."

The honest sweeper went on his way happy with his thirty

gold coins and grateful to God for the wisdom and fairness of the Sultan. For his part, the dishonest merchant returned glumly to his affairs, lamenting the loss of his thirty gold coins but powerless to reclaim them because of his sworn declaration and the Sultan's decree.

Doña Francisca's Dress

Of the Spanish aristocracy still residing in Mexico after independence from Spain in 1824 none was more beloved of the common people of Mexico City than Countess Francisca de Braganza, widow of Don Caspar de la Huerta y Figueroa. The elder sister of one of the last Spanish viceroys in Mexico, she not only outlived her wealthy husband and famous brother Don Miguel . . . but imperial Spanish hegemony as well. Many Spaniards returned to Spain when the war of liberation severed links with the mother country. But others, including Doña Francisca, remained in the Aztec Republic, bound by commercial ties and family sentiments that after many years of residence in Mexico were now more Mexican than Spanish.

Always generous and charitable toward the less fortunate of the great capital, Doña Francisca became even more lavish in her donations after her husband's death in 1825. She contributed to every good cause and no few bad ones. In this philanthropic endeavor she received guidance and advice from Father Domingo Olmedo of the Franciscan Order. Though still young, he was admired throughout the great city for his inspirational homilies, sage advice to his parishioners, and not least, his remarkable physical handsomeness. Perhaps with dubious motives in some cases, many high-born ladies prevailed on him to be their spiritual mentor.

But if Doña Francisca was among those who sought him, there was no question about the pure caliber of her faith and philanthropy. Nor was her largesse dispensed at an abstract remove from the populace. Often, she would order the driver to stop her carriage in busy avenues and send him with food or coinage to help the hungry and destitute she saw on her daily rides about the city. Her fame spread widely among the poor, and crowds of beggars followed her carriage with piteous clamoring and scuffling for alms while her harassed driver tried to negotiate his way through the ravening horde. Indeed, the motley mob at times pressed so forcefully against the carriage that it was in danger of toppling over. These scenes horrified her family, but Doña Francisca herself enjoyed the tumult and smiled beatifically through the raucous scenes.

Her children, Don Plácido de la Huerta y Braganza and Doña Matilde de la Huerta de Vela, were distressed by her largesse, fearing that she would dissipate her fortune and leave them penniless and socially *déclassé*. And even though her friends loved Doña Francisca, they also complained privately that her indiscriminate handouts were creating public nuisances by emboldening the beggars to form a veritable host of aggressive undesirables. Indeed, rumors spread that even persons of adequate means dressed themselves as beggars to take advantage of the grand dowager's generosity.

But mercifully, before she could reduce the family to penury and the aristocratic district around the Alameda Park to turmoil, Doña Francisca died peacefully in her sleep in 1833, a few days past her ninety-fifth birthday. Whereupon Doña Matilde quickly shed misgivings about her saintly mother's legendary generosity and determined to honor her memory with the most elaborate funeral imaginable. Like mother now like daughter, for she had also came to depend on Father Olmedo for spiritual guidance and counsel.

Crowning the funeral pomp and ceremony was the extraordinary dress Doña Francisca wore to her grave, the same one the grand lady had donned as a bride on her wedding day many decades earlier in the golden age of the Mexican viceroyalty. The dress was the epitome of luxury such as high fashion decreed in Doña Francisca' s distant youth. It was a metaphor of wealth and creativity, the acme of earthly beauty set to vie against mortality's implacable destructive tide. To the elegance of French Enlightenment style was added the baroque splendor of Mexican opulence: bows cunningly bordered with gold; silver pendants, broches, and bracelets; gold rings inlaid with precious stones, a pearl necklace worth a king's ransom; a bejeweled tiara that not even Aladdin's magical genie could have surpassed, and, finally, the costliest accompanying laces, diamonds, rubies, emeralds, and sapphires.

Thus, amidst an opulence that beggars description, Doña Matilde sent Countess Francisca to her eternal reward like an Egyptian pharaoh supplied with enough riches, so it would appear, to live eternally in full magnificence, seemingly giving lie to the hackneyed saying that the deceased can take no worldly riches with them into the Hereafter. By all accounts, it was the most extraordinary funeral in the history of Mexico City.

Father Olmedo gave it his full blessing: "Such extraordinary outpourings of piety and generosity ought always to be held up as worthy examples for all believers to emulate as their means allow," he told Doña Matilde and Don Plácido. "In this way, you shall make it possible for our beloved Countess Francisca to inspire in death what she did so nobly in life."

Thus bedecked in unsurpassable splendor, Countess Francisca lay in state in her casket as thousands of mourners bade her a sad but glorious farewell. Father Olmedo's funeral eulogy was a thing of pathos and beauty that left not a soul unmoved, nor hardly a dry eye in the cathedral. Her passing was more than a personal death, he reminded them. "With her," he said with surpassing eloquence to the weeping mourners, "there has passed away an age of grace and grandeur such as the world has never seen before and may never see again."

Then her casket was conveyed before the teary multitudes to her tomb, and after burial and dispersal of the last mourners, the sexton locked the family mausoleum and pocketed the key.

*****

Although Dona Francisca's exemplary life and all it signified was over, her story was not yet finished. Hear now its final chapter.

Almost coincidental with Doña Francisca's extraordinary funeral, a traveling company of French ballerinas performed in Mexico City. Though perhaps not of the first rank by European standards, the company's lead ballerina was famous for her exciting pirouettes and the brevity of her attire, which allowed more provocative glimpses of flesh than Mexican custom of that era sanctioned. Hence the public's eager anticipation of the performance. And as if this enticement were not enough, the spicy rumor circulated that not only had she danced before European royalty but also had performed in more intimate ways with certain princes.

True to form, she made her stage entry with a series of extravagant spins and twists. Then prancing across the stage on tiptoe she looked at the audience, awaiting their applause. But instead of an ovation, there arose a murmur of horror and not a few boos from the indignant public. For there before their very eyes danced Mademoiselle Marie Sabouret, she of dubious fame, clad not in her customary brief attire but wearing the bejeweled dress in which saintly Countess Francisca was buried!

As soon as the final curtain fell, police authorities surrounded the defiant and indignant Mlle. Sabouret and escorted her offstage for interrogation. Where and how did you come by this dress? they asked her. She insisted that she bought it with her own money—a not inconsiderable amount of her money—at a French dressmaker's shop in Mexico City. She had disturbed no grave, she vehemently declared, and was horrified by the very thought of such a sacrilegious act. Next the police authorities questioned the dressmaker. She also claimed total innocence in the matter and swore she had bought the dress from a man who brought it to her shop. Describe the man, they ordered her. Fairly young, she told them, thirtyish perhaps, tall, well-dressed, with the manners and speech of a high-born person. She surmised that he was well educated, for at one point where her Spanish was deficient, he addressed her in perfect French. When they asked about his features, she demurred and said that they were half hidden by a cowl or hood. Tell us, they ordered her, what you recall about his face, any details that might be of use. Tentatively, she described not his features, but suppositions based on the few indirect glimpses she had of them. Handsome, she supposed intuitively, and uncharacteristically cleanshaven. Beyond that she could tell them nothing except that his fingers were exceptionally long and his hands white and delicate, almost dainty, and now that she thought about it, not those of a man used to normal manual tasks. Perhaps the hands of an aristocrat or an artist, she speculated.

The authorities had already settled tentatively on a suspect: the cathedral sexton. But the dressmaker's words did not support that hypothesis. Still, he could be implicated, and they proceeded to interrogate him. The sexton, by name López, was of middling age and his hands were brown and calloused from rough labor, anything but delicate. Yet he seemed so nervous that the authorities immediately deduced by his behavior an undetermined degree of culpability.

"Tell us your part in this crime," the police captain demanded. "We know you are involved. Did you desecrate the tomb to steal the items in question? Better you tell us the truth, for you stand in grave danger of execution by firing squad," the captain said as he jerked the kneeling man erect to stare him in the face.

The sexton shook as though palsied.

"Mercy! Mercy!" he cried. "I bear no blame in the matter you describe, sir!"

"There is no mercy for those who desecrate tombs. Confess your crime, wretch, and appeal to God for mercy, for you shall have none when we turn you over to the magistrate for sentencing!"

"But, sir, I was ordered to do what I did. And I had to obey him who gave the order."

"Then you opened the grave?"

"I had to obey his order or forfeit my livelihood and my soul besides. I have a wife and children. I had no choice in the matter."

"Miserable dog, who ordered you to desecrate the grave?"

"Sir, I cannot say. On pain of eternal condemnation, I cannot say!" responded, shaking his head in terror and despair.

The captain conferred for a moment with his officers, then

spoke in a softer tone. "Then the man who gave you the order is a person of authority?"

The trembling sexton nodded.

"And he threatened to harm you if you did not obey his order?"

Again, he nodded.

"And what was to be the punishment for your disobedience?"

The trembling sexton hesitated.

"Tell us or torture to loosen your tongue will begin now."

"Sir, he told me that if I did not obey his order he would condemn my soul to hell!"

"And you believed him?"

"Yes, sir."

"And why did you believe him?"

"Because he could, sir."

"Aha! Now we're getting somewhere. Then this man you speak of has the power, or claims to have it, to cast your soul into hell forever?"

"He does, sir."

"We are speaking, then, of a priest, are we not?"

The sexton nodded and hung his head.

"His name. Tell us his name."

"I cannot, sir."

"Then tell us at least this, you wicked sexton. Is the priest assigned to the cathedral?"

"I cannot say, sir."

"You will say soon enough when we torture the words out of you. But for now, men, lock him in a cell so that he cannot take refuge in the Cathedral. We shall loosen his tongue when the red-hot irons pierce his eyes. I promise you, sexton, you shall have a foretaste of the hell you dread before we are finished with you this night."

The sexton blanched and shook with terror. "Mercy! Mercy! I beg you! I will tell you the name. Only do not blind me! I will tell you the name!"

"Then tell on. My patience wears thin and the hot irons will be next if you do not confess.""

"Father Olmedo, sir! It was Father Olmedo!" he gasped. "He said he would condemn my soul to hell if I did not open the grave. Never before have I done such an unholy thing, sir. I respect the dead. But he swore to condemn my soul to hell!"

"So, Father Olmedo desecrated the tomb and took the dress?"

"And the precious gems, gold, and all things of value and profit, sir."

"And what did you accept for your part in this unholy act?"

"Nothing, nothing I swear, sir! Never in a million years would I rob the dead. I am a faithful servant of the Church, but I had no choice, sir. If I had not obeyed him, he would have . . ."

"I know, you have said it too many times tonight. Men, lock this ignorant fool in a cell until we can deal with him as his crime deserves. Then meet me here. We have a greater scoundrel to confront."

"Sir, I have told you all I know. Will you deal kindly with me?"

"I shall not deal at all with you, but you may sure that the magistrate will hand down such justice as your crime deserves."

The captain and his men were grimly aware that they could not arrest a priest within cathedral precincts should he invoke the hallowed principle of religious sanctuary. But at least they could confront the author of an unthinkable crime against everything holy. In these cases, canon law prevailed, and indeed might apply also to the ignorant sexton if his part in the crime was brought to the attention of church authorities. In any case, they were more concerned with the mastermind behind the sacrilegious outrage and could only hope that the Bishop and above him, the Archbishop, would cooperate to punish Olmedo severely for his sacrilege.

But as it turned out there was to be no confrontation. Father Olmedo had vanished without a trace when the captain and his men reached the Cathedral. He was never seen again in Mexico City. A rumor quickly spread and long persisted that he had "hung up his habit," as the saying goes, in exchange for the carnal favors of Mademoiselle Sabouret. What truth, if any, there was to the rumor remained a matter of speculation.

*****

Post Script: A granddaughter of Doña Francisca said years later that she and her husband were pestered by a filthy beggar at the entrance to Notre Dame Cathedral in Paris, and learning from their speech that they were Mexican, to their surprise he told them in perfect Spanish how many years earlier as a young man he had been a celebrated priest in Mexico City until he yielded to carnal temptations. Now having repented of his sins, but still paying the worldly consequences of his wrongdoing, he begged them most piteously for alms. They scoffed at his claims and rejected his pleas, knowing that hunger spurs beggars to spin wondrous lies for bread and drink. Thus, the truth of his claim, if any there be, remained unverified.

A second rumor about Father Olmedo arose and circulated briefly in the capital. According to it, a renegade priest perhaps with the same surname was imprisoned in a town in the far north of the Republic. He managed to escape before he could be tried. The rumor gained little credence and soon died away. As countless members of high Mexican society well knew, Father Olmedo as a sophisticate addicted to luxury, fine cuisine, and the arts. It would be unthinkable that a man of his tastes would seek refuge on the untamed northern frontier with its wild Apaches and Comanches, ignorant peasants, and barbaric Americans. It was far more likely, they agreed, that Olmedo would find a way to get to Europe, probably France.

But the story of Doña Francisca's fabulous dress has a more verifiable ending than either rumor. It was Doña Matilde's hope that her mother's tomb might be opened a second time in order to drape the fabulous dress across her mother's remains. Father Suárez, the local priest and Olmedo's replacement, agreed to the request, but the newly appointed young Bishop, born in a new century and a new age, overruled him. He declared that the dress was a symbol of sinful pride of life that corrupted the moral structure of the civilized world in the so-called Age of Enlightenment orchestrated by Voltaire.

"Lock the dress away in the bowels of the Cathedral," he ordered Father Suárez, "and do not let parishioners regard it again. Any virtue associated with it in the lifetime of Countess Francisca has been tainted by the evil purposes to which sinful men turned it. I shall inform the Archbishop in due course of my decision, and unless he should decide otherwise, the matter is settled."

Thus, it was done and thus the decree remained in force. In time knowledge of the dress passed out of living memory and into the realm of legend.

The Murderer's Tale

(From "Memoirs of a Renegade Priest")

After the disastrous events that led to my precipitous flight from Mexico City, I sought to conceal myself in a remote northern province of the Mexican Republic, a land of cold winters and colder hearts which the Americans later seized and made of it a nation. My natural desire was to make my way back to dear France, there to resume, if possible, the happier days of my youth. But I suppressed the impulse, reasoning that my best chance for survival lay in taking a direction that my pursuers would least expect. The strategy worked and once in this remote land, though disgraced, exhausted, and lamenting my fall from grace, my fortunes quickly improved. For several months I prospered materially, posing as a priest when the opportunity presented itself in the most improbable way possible. In other ways, however, I was lonely and depressed to a state bordering on despair in my limited circumstances.

I recall that I had spent, or better said, wasted, a dull April afternoon thinking of my plight and dispensing my usual false absolutions to repentant old women for their malicious gossip and vulgar disputes. Because so few men confessed, and then only for more interesting and lascivious reasons, I took more than usual notice when a man who looked to be above fifty years began his confession with these words:

"Father, I have killed a man and I would tell you in confession the why and how of the deed and ask for forgiveness, if you would hear me."

His words produced a nervous shock in me and I sat bolt upright. There, only inches away, were the lean, rough hands of a man who had done another to death. From the confessional I stared at the side of his face, visible in the shadows, trying to discover in his features some revealing feature that separated him from common men. The practiced words dropped mechanically from my lips:

"Confess your misdeeds, my son, for God forgives those who truly repent of their sins. *Ave María Purísima.*"

"*Sin pecado concebida.* Willingly I confess them, Father, though repentance is a harder matter, as you will understand when you hear my story."

Perceiving that his confession promised to be longer and more entertaining than the mindless squawking of the usual rabble, I bade him step into my office where he could speak privately without eavesdroppers or disturbances. He thanked me and in a tone that betrayed a soul much acquainted with suffering, told me the following tale:

My name, Father, is Mariano Otero. I was born and lived my early life on the prosperous hacienda of don Cayetano Aranda y Toledo. It spread for several leagues along both banks of the Nazas River as it flows west from Torreón. For many generations, my family had served the Arandas loyally as *charros* (ranch workers) and *capataces* (foremen): father replaced grandfather, and son succeeded father in a proud, unbroken line. The Arandas repaid the loyalty of all their workers with Christian charity and affection, ministering to them during illness, providing a school for their children, and giving gifts for saint's days and first communions. In truth we loved and respected them with a devotion that rose above our differences of class and station in the world.

Nowhere was this hereditary bond between our families warmer or more evident than in the friendship that united me to Alvaro Luis Aranda y Flores, the only son of don Cayetano and his wife doña Catalina Flores de Aranda. As we grew up together, I was fiercely proud to walk and ride beside him and hear him tell others of our friendship. Willingly I would have put my hands in the fire for him, so great was my devotion and gratitude. For, in truth, our gifts were greatly unequal. He was taller and stronger than I, though we were near in age to each other, and as a horseman and marksman, he had no peer in all the haciendas of that country, nor could any youth match him in demonstrations of strength and daring. In contrast to the stern and morally correct don Cayetano, Alvaro, who was as handsome as his mother doña Catalina was beautiful, soon gained further fame as an irresistible seducer and many stories were told of his conquests of maidens and married women alike.

I, on the other hand, was only passably adequate in the skills expected of a *capataz* and *charro* and entirely wanting in the qualities for winning the fair sex. Yet my father taught me the former with patience such that, in time, I overcame my awkwardness and achieved a level of competence that don Cayetano himself saw fit to praise. It was a matter of great pride for our family to hear him acclaim me as the worthy successor to my ancestors and future foreman of the hacienda. But, as to the latter qualities I spoke of, they were beyond my father's ability to teach, and I remained as timid and tongue-tied as ever when it came to *señoritas*.

Disturbed by Alvaro's many amorous scandals and dangerous escapades and seeking to curb and discipline his reckless nature, in 1806 don Cayetano sent his eighteen-year-old son to study in Mexico City and then abroad to complete his education and acquaint him with the civilizing cultures of Europe. For nearly six years I barely saw Alvaro at all. From time to time, in response to our inquiries, don Cayetano would relay news about him sent from Madrid, Paris, or Rome.

Meanwhile, despite my clumsiness with women, I met and fell in love with Guadalupe Mendoza. She was the shy, pretty seventeen-year-old daughter of don Marcelino Mendoza y Carranza, a retired and widowed Torreón judge who shared a passion for the chase with don Cayetano and often came to the hacienda for hunting trips to the sierra. Because doña Catalina had no daughters of her own, she persuaded don Marcelino to leave her goddaughter in her care on those occasions so that she might spoil her with gifts, dresses, and the maternal affection that only a woman could offer.

Having led a cloistered life in a convent school in Torreón in complete innocence of the outer world, Lupita, as everybody called her, thrilled to the newly discovered beauties of nature and often asked permission to take long carriage rides through the hacienda and surrounding countryside. Always ready to indulge her but often unable because of household responsibilities to accompany her charge, doña Catalina asked me to escort Lupita in these excursions.

It is unnecessary, Father, to describe to you the profound impress that Lupita's innocent charms and joyous nature made on my heart. She was able with a look or a word to dispel my grave disposition and bring an unused smile to my lips. Suffice it to say that I fell so completely in love with her that no other woman would ever hold any appeal for me. So strong, indeed, was my love that eventually it overcame my customary shyness and our differences of class and I confessed my feelings to her and my earnest desire to be her husband.

She reacted with surprise, nay, more, with astonishment, Father, for such sentiments were as yet unknown to her. Withal, she responded nobly and sincerely, as was her wont, that although she esteemed and trusted me as a dear friend, she did not feel the love for me that she read of in books or heard as gossip from other girls. She protested that class differences meant nothing to her and that her respect for me was limitless.

I was not discouraged by her rejection of my proposal but, instead, deemed myself highly favored to be counted as her friend. I did not again mention my amorous feelings but rather redoubled my courteous and respectful attentions and sought in every way to merit her high regard. As time passed and our friendship deepened, she confided her feelings, especially concerns for her father's health.

These worries were not unfounded. As her eighteenth birthday approached, the venerable don Marcelino took to his deathbed. His one remaining worldly concern was for Lupita's welfare, and he regretted to leave her alone without the affection and protection of a good husband. Thereupon, she dutifully made known to him my feelings for her. At first don Marcelino expressed misgivings about my inferior standing, but upon receiving assurances from don Cayetano concerning my character, loyalty, and my family's modest but solid material holdings, forthwith he became my advocate and gave his blessings to our union. To our great sorrow, only days thereafter he expired with full rites of the Church and comforting reassurances from the weeping don Cayetano and doña Catalina that henceforth Lupita would live at the hacienda, where she would be loved and wedded to me as their own daughter.

Alas, Father, what man proposes to his happiness oft goes awry to his misery. At that fateful moment in 1812, the long absent Alvaro returned from his travels. Taller and more handsome than we remembered him, to his native charm he added Old World sophistication and flourish. His parents were delighted and don Cayetano, himself rapidly declining in strength and health, thought only of turning over the affairs of the hacienda to his prodigal son. As for doña Catalina, she hoped to see him promptly married and dreamed optimistically of numerous grandchildren.

As fate would have it, therefore, Alvaro and Lupita coincided in their arrival at the hacienda. No sooner had they met than Alvaro, indifferent to my prior claims to her heart and more polished and proficient than ever in the seductive arts, at once commenced to bedazzle her. Within days she became distant and distracted in our conversations. I pressed her as to the reason for her change of mood, and unable to dissemble, she tearfully confessed her love for Alvaro, adding, however, that out of loyalty to me and in obedience to her late father's instructions, she intended to honor her promise to marry me.

With a broken heart, I offered to stand aside. At first Lupita was unwilling to see me suffer. In her distraught state she sought the counsel of doña Catalina who, in her anxiety to see her volatile son settled in marriage, ignored my plight and advised Lupita to accept Alvaro instead. Returning to me with this advice, she asked permission to end her betrothal. I granted her wish, pledging my friendship and help, if ever she should have need of them.

They were wed, and less than a year later, Lupita gave birth to a daughter, Raquel, as beautiful as herself. They honored me with a request to be her godfather.

At first Alvaro was devoted to Lupita, and despite my personal pain, I took pleasure in witnessing their happiness from afar. But soon Alvaro began to slip back into his old vices, now made worse by his scorn for our provincial ways. Before many months had passed, he tired of Lupita and his daughter and began drinking and gambling in the local taverns. Gossip commenced to circulate of new mistresses.

This unhappy news and Alvaro's wanton behavior, which in every aspect was alien to his own high code of conduct, hastened don Cayetano's decline, and before two more years had passed, we mourned his death as the loyal friend and generous patriarch he had always been. Nor did doña Catalina long survive him. Distressed by the loss of her husband and driven to near insanity by the scandalous behavior of her son, she soon took her place beside don Cayetano in the cemetery.

Thereupon Alvaro dropped all pretense of responsibility and began an orgy of drinking and dissipation. The hacienda was soon mortgaged and jeopardized, for even though my father and I tried our best to maintain it, we could not staunch the financial drain caused by Alvaro's excesses. We lost most of our own money in the futile effort.

Lupita was mortified and humiliated by her husband's brutal, abusive behavior and cynical disregard of the family's welfare. Determined to be true to my promise, I befriended her in every decent way I could and lavished attention on the shy and reserved Raquelita as though she were my own daughter. In truth, I looked on her as such, for she was the daughter I would never have and Lupita, the wife I would never call my own.

Despite our efforts, not many years passed before the hacienda came to utter ruin and creditors came forth to seize it from drunken Alvaro. The neighboring haciendas could offer me no work, for the war against Spain had devasted our region. So with great sadness I announced to Lupita that I must leave Torreón to seek my livelihood elsewhere. My own father was now in decline and too broken in body and spirit to accompany me. I made provisions for him to live near my married sister Francisca in Chihuahua and, with a heavy heart, left the high country of Torreón and drifted to the tropical land of Chiapas, where I worked for many years on a coffee plantation. After a few years I received word from Francisca that my father had died. I wrote often to Lupita and Raquelita and treasured their responses, though unlike her mother, shy Raquelita wrote but sparingly. Then after a few years, their letters ceased altogether, and I had no more news of them.

Twelve years passed before I was able, by hard work and frugal hoarding of my earnings, to leave Chiapas and return to my ancestral Torreón. What I found there, Father, was a thing unbelievable though, on my mother's honor, I swear to its truthfulness.

The hacienda was vastly changed, and its present owner did not welcome my inquiries. To my questions about Alvaro Aranda he sneered that I should seek him in the streets and taverns of Torreón. There, indeed, I found him, but in the most wretched state imaginable. The once princely Alvaro, now consumed by alcohol, shuffled and shook as he begged abjectly for money in the street. He seemed not to recognize me when I spoke to him, but his once handsome face twisted into a travesty of his brilliant smile when I deposited coins in his proffered cup, for his teeth were gone and his jaws shrunken.

"Mariano?" he lisped blankly. "Mariano Otero, you say? That is a name I seem to recall. I have known you somewhere, friend, long ago perhaps in a different and better time. Invite me to a drink and surely my memory will return. My memory revives after a drink."

We sat and drank, and indeed he seemed to remember me after a time. But though he recalled a few of our boyhood adventures, he turned evasive when I asked him about Lupita and Raquelita. Abruptly he cursed me for meddling in his affairs and staggered out of the tavern. I turned in bewilderment to the tavern owner, who rolled his eyes in disgust.

"I overheard your name and remember your father, Señor Otero, and it is a name still respected in Torreón. Only out of respect for you and your father, Señor, have I allowed Alvaro Aranda to drink in my establishment at all. For he is a man who deserves no consideration or, for that matter, does not deserve to live!"

"That is a harsh thing to say, my friend. It seems odd that you, a taverner, should so condemn one whom the bottle has bested."

"I do not say the thing for his vice but for the much greater guilt he bears."

"And what is that?"

"You have indeed been long absent from this city not to have heard what he did to his wife and daughter."

I rose from my chair and confronted the man, who mistook my anxiety for anger.

"Do not be angry with me, Señor. I am only repeating what is common knowledge in Torreón. Ask anybody and they will tell you the same."

"The same 'what'? What did he do to his family?"

"Ah, Señor, it is the saddest of stories. When Alvaro lost the hacienda, the family began a life of poverty. They took a dilapidated room in Torreón and the lady Lupita and her daughter lived for a time on the generosity of the Sisters of Charity, and a few loyal friends. But Alvaro seized all they were given and used it to continue his drinking and gambling. Soon the friends tired of Lupita and the Sisters refused to give them more aid for Alvaro to squander. Now, indeed, they were reduced to utter misery.

"It was then that Alvaro ordered them into the streets to beg. At long last, the meek doña Lupita refused. But in his insane rage, Alvar gave is wife a savage beating, as he often did, and then, if the rumors be true, sold the sixteen-year-old Raquelita to a house of prostitution. There, I was told, she was actioned to wealthy bidders, the winner paying a handsome sum for the privilege of deflowering her. Within weeks, they say, she was taken to Mexico City and no one has seen or heard of her since.

"The pain and shame of it drove Lupita mad. For years, she wandered the streets of Torreón calling for Raquelita. Malicious children tormented her in the street and people threw her scraps to eat and rags to cover her back, but Alvaro mocked her madness. Finally, they found her body in an alley and buried it in a pauper's grave. And as surely as my name is Jorge Castellano, Señor, that is why I will not permit Alvaro Aranda to enter my establishment, not if he had all the money in Torreón."

I left the tavern in a red, trembling rage, determined to find

Alvaro and avenge Lupita and Raquelita. But as I walked the streets in search of the monster, I thought better of my unpremeditated plan to strangle him on the spot. For why should I go to prison, perhaps to my death, for killing a man who, it was commonly agreed, did not deserve to live? Instead, I purchased a bottle of cheap wine, opened it, poured in a generous quantity of arsenic, and replaced the cork. Then I searched the streets until I found Alvaro begging at one of his accustomed spots. He eyed me warily until I offered him the bottle with this warning:

"Alvaro, you may have this wine if you wish, but I warn you it contains a poison and you will die if you drink it."

With a curse, he grabbed the bottle, glared at me for a moment with a malicious hint of his former intelligence, and muttered as he fumbled to pop the cork, "I have been dead a long time anyway, Mariano."

With that he flipped the cork aside and took a long gurgling draught, his throat pumping rhythmically as he drank. Shortly thereafter he fell to the ground and began to twitch and convulse as curious onlookers gathered to watch him die. So ended Alvaro and with him the proud, illustrious Aranda line.

The authorities conducted only the briefest of inquiries into the cause of death. Had not doctors warned him many times that drink would kill him? But, Father, they never knew the truth I tell you now, for if there was gossip that I had a hand in his death, it did not reach their ears, or mine.

I paid for his funeral out of respect for his parents and the early memories I had of him. Lupita's tomb was unknown, so I could only have a mass said for the eternal rest of her soul. Despite my efforts, I have been unable to find my goddaughter Raquelita. Yet I continue to search for her, pursuing one phantom rumor after another. For I love her like a father and, for my beloved Lupita's sake, would give my life for her.

"And that, Father, is why and how I killed a man, and why now I seek forgiveness for my sin."

For a moment, I sat in stunned silence at the revelation I had just heard. Then remembering my expected response, I gave him absolution, lecturing on the gravity of his crime but requiring for penance for the deed only that he surrender something of value. He offered a solid gold cross, which I accepted in the name of the Church of the Good Shepherd and, naturally, kept for myself.

Raquelita's Revenge

(From "Memoirs of a Renegade Priest")

By a calamitous turn of events, a feature that seems to describe my wretched life, my lucrative charade as a priest was discovered, and on the Bishop's order I was imprisoned in San Cristóbal de los Frailes, located in a desolate, mountainous land with barely any intercourse with civilization. Months passed in friendless solitude and fear that word of my earlier chicaneries in Mexico City would reach authorities in the north. For had they discovered my unpleasant antecedents to add to my present misdeeds, no doubt I would have been summarily executed by firing squad. I had all but given up hope of freedom when an equally strange and improbable series of incidents worked to my rescue. Thereafter I rode with the Bernardo Aguirre outlaws for a season, hoping my fortunes would take a better turn and miraculously restore me to the comforts and pleasures of my former life. On one occasion, as we rested between raids, entertaining ourselves with music, food, wine, and wondrous tales, Raquelita, Bernardo's mistress and the only woman in the band, told me the following tale, indicating that although she knew I was not, or no longer, a priest, she wanted to unburden herself by telling her story, trusting that from habit I would respect her confidentiality. None but I knew its startling connection to an earlier confession whispered in my ear, and among such volatile and dangerous men the reader may be sure that I kept the knowledge to myself at least until my ties to the outlaws were abruptly and definitively cut not long afterward. But all that is another much longer story. These are her words:

I was born in Torreón and spent my earliest years on our spacious and prosperous hacienda, inherited from my paternal grandfather don Cayetano Aranda. My father, Alvaro, was his only son and my mother, Guadalupe Mendoza, the only child of Magistrate Marcelino Mendoza. All my grandparents died before I had memory of them, but the many stories told of their noble character and admirable generosity filled me with a posthumous love for them and a fierce pride in my ancestry. Descended on both sides from ancient Spanish nobility, since the earliest days of New Spain they were among its foremost families.

Upon his return in 1812 after five or six years of study, travel, and adventures in Europe, he who was destined to be my father was acclaimed the most handsome young bachelor in the whole region of Torreón. He stirred the hearts and raised the hopes of every marriageable señorita for many leagues around. But from the moment he cast eyes on my mother, his heart was captivated by her beauty and they were soon wed.

But now I must introduce into these happy circumstances the despicable Mariano Otero, a vile monster of a man who was to inflict fatal evil on my family. Not long before my father returned from his years abroad, Otero had dared to propose matrimony to my mother, even though as a mere worker and Charro on our hacienda, he was in every way inferior to her in class and standing. Her father had given his deathbed blessing to the union, but her godmother, my grandmother, doña Catalina, dismissed his approval as evidence of his diminished reason. Outwardly cordial to Otero, secretly she contemplated the proposed marriage with horror and persuaded her to dismiss him and accept my father instead.

Otero pretended to accept graciously my mother's decision to break her betrothal, but as I was to learn later, from that very hour he conceived a murderous hatred for my father and behind his back did all in his power to harm him. Yet so skillfully did he ingratiate himself with my parents that they named him godfather to me and held him to be their most trusted friend.

This close intercourse with our family afforded him many chances to worm his way deeper into my mother's confidence. He hovered about her, solicitous traitor that he was, ever ready to do her bidding. No favor was too small or large for him to do for her, no compliment too insignificant for him to pay her. Pretending to be my father's devoted friend, he availed himself of every opportunity to make innuendoes touching on his flaws and slyly to impress on my mother's vulnerable mind the evil notion that he was unworthy of her love and trust.

Otero was abetted in his diabolical scheme by my mother's jealous nature, for no sooner did he hint of my father's infidelities than she took them to be fact. In truth, however, my father was devoted to her and so startled and bewildered by her screaming accusations that, in time, he came to question her sanity and, worse, to doubt her love for him.

Sadly, these confrontations and damning suspicions became more frequent and violent. Finding no hope of remedy for her outbursts, my disillusioned father took to gambling he evenings away in the taverns. Soon, his drinking was noticeable, and rumors circulated of other women. Too late my mother commenced to realize the folly of her insane jealousy and promised time and again to change her behavior. But her native disposition and Otero's insinuations were too strong, and as she failed to curb her rages, alcoholism and gambling consumed my father.

Grieving over their unhappy son's vices, my grandparents soon declined and departed this life. The hacienda then passed into my father's hands, but so ravaged was he by the bottle that he neglected its maintenance and devoted himself entirely to squandering its resources.

Meanwhile, Otero and his father, both cut from the same rotten fabric, plotted to gain possession of the hacienda. In this scheme, however, more adroit creditors outsmarted them. If there was any bitter satisfaction in the events that ensured, it was in knowing that, in the end, Otero fell into the very trap they had laid for my family.

To the great consternation of my parents, from my earliest childhood I detested Mariano Otero. For all that he was my godfather and sought to win me with gifts and obsequious attentions, I loathed him for reasons I could not explain. Some say that children can sense the true character of a person. That may be so, but I suspect—and sometimes can nearly recall—that in my infancy I heard or saw unremembered things that shaped my morbid impressions of him. It was only under pressure by my parents that I suffered his company at all. There were many unpleasant disputes between us as they labored to convince me of his goodness and I, to persuade them of his duplicity.

As my father sank deeper into alcoholism, my mother idealized her old feelings for Otero. In truth she had never loved him, yet now she gilded their friendship—for that was all it ever was—with such fantasies that she no longer remembered the difference. Then she began to draw unfavorable comparisons betwixt husband and suitor, and these tilted so in favor of the latter that she lamented aloud and to my father's face the mistaken choice she had made.

I was still a child, no more than ten, when utter ruin finally overtook us. Three somber officials in black attire and top hats came in a carriage to seize the hacienda with official documents and legal pronouncements. It was a day I shall never forget, though on my oath, I would gladly give all the gold I have stolen to erase the bitter memory from my mind.

With the help of an old friend of my late grandfather, we took up residence—if it can be called that—in a miserable hovel in Torreón. There we subsisted for time on the charity of the Sisters and the handouts of our remaining friends. But before long they tired of us and ceased their help, pointing to my father's drinking as the reason. In truth, our friends were few to start with, for no sooner had word spread of our disgrace than, without ado, most turned their back on us. I cannot describe the shame and mortification I suffered as girls who once were my best friends now, on the instructions of their parents, refused to speak to me or mocked me openly in the streets.

Then even the obsequious Otero abandoned us. Instead of befriending my parents and seeing to their welfare as he sworn to do as my godfather, he announced to us that he and his father were leaving Torreón. He promised to help us as soon as he was established elsewhere, and for many months both my parents, but especially my mother, vainly awaited news from him. "The good Mariano will not abandon us. He will send help soon," she repeated. Yet all we received from him were long tasteless responses to our letters in which he described his homesickness in Chiapas but made only scant references to our circumstances. Never was there any material aid or hint of help.

When it finally became evident to my parents that their last hope had failed them, their spirits broke and our family collapsed completely. One night, as my mother commenced her daily tribute to Otero, my father, drunk as usual, suddenly rose from his chair and with a great bellowing cry, gave her a brutal beating, despite my efforts to stop him.

Neither of them recovered. My mother's reason began to evaporate and, ere long, she became insensible to reality. Eventually her physical wounds healed, but there were many times when she seemed no longer able to recognize even me. Often, she slipped out of the house to wander as a vagrant about the city until I would find her and lead her home. As for my father, crazed by grief and drink, he shed the last pretense of shame and became a drunken street beggar.

I was left alone and desperate, without means or friends. At sixteen, the only assets I had left were my youthful looks and body. These I sold at a brothel, and as a prostitute, I took perverse pleasure in bedding the husbands and suitors of my former friends. Upon hearing of my degradation, my father summoned a spark of his former dignity and attempted to rescue me from the brothel. It pains me to remember that I laughed him to scorn and threw up to him his many failings. In the end, he hung his head and disappeared — though not before asking me for money. So bereft of reason my mother had become that I am certain she never knew what became of me.

Because I was much sought out by the men of Torreón, soon I had enough money to leave the city and the bitter memories it held for me. My parents were beyond rescue in any case, and all my thoughts were fixed on flying from the brutal humiliations I had suffered. One of my wealthy clients offered to establish me in a residence in the capital of the Republic, provided I reserve my favors for him. I agreed to his conditions and he took me to

Mexico City. There I prospered, for besides the monthly allowance he faithfully gave me, during his frequent absences I earned more plying my lucrative profession.

In this way, eight years passed, and my elderly protector died. I mourned his death with genuine regret, for he was always kind. Indeed, towards the end I came to look on him more as a kindly uncle than a lover.

Thanks to his generosity and my own enterprise I had, by then, accumulated a tidy sum and my thoughts increasingly turned to Torreón and my parents. Furthermore, during the liquidation of my lover's property, his family learned of my secret residence in Mexico City and demanded my removal. I left willingly and without scandal, for I had tired of my life there and hoped to establish myself in the provinces.

In Torreón I learned the sad news of my mother's demise. You may imagine the remorse I felt for having abandoned her. But my regret turned to outrage when I learned that only a few weeks earlier Mariano Otero also had returned to Torreón and according to rumors, as a final act of hatred towards my father, had murdered him with a bottle of poisoned wine. He had the effrontery to pay for his burial. But rather than have my father lie in a tomb of infamy, I paid for his reburial in the Aranda mausoleum. No one knew where they had buried my mother. All I could do was to have a mass said in her name. Imagine my rage when they told me the hypocritical Otero had requested a similar mass for her. Otero, the very man responsible for her ruin and death!

That same day I swore vengeance and commenced to pursue Otero, as a hunter would stalk a wild beast, with the intention of killing him without the least hesitation. First I followed him to

Chihuahua, then to San Cristóbal de los Frailes, only to learn that he had departed not long since for San Antonio. There, in the distant north, at last I found him as he sat drinking alone in a tavern. So changed was I that at first he failed to recognize me as I called his name. It was only when I came near enough to plunge my knife into his black heart that his eyes widened in recognition.

"Why, dear Raquelita, why?" were his dying words said barely above a whisper.

Why indeed! As if he did not know that I had reasons to kill him a hundred times over!

Because Otero was a stranger without consequence or connections in San Antonio, the authorities readily accepted my claim that his death was just retribution for a great dishonor done to my family and me. They asked only that I leave San Antonio. Having extracted vengeance, I departed at once, and following the pathway that destiny set before me, eventually threw my lot in with Bernardo.

I was curious to know which version of the story was the truer, hers or Otero's. I had believed his story when I heard it several months earlier, but now hers also had the persuasive ring of truth. But when I tried to question her further, she ignored me. "I would not ask her more questions," Bernardo whispered to me. "It can be dangerous to press her. She speaks only when she will, and her rage is often sudden and violent. The man who destroyed her family is not the only one who has died by her hand. She will tell you more only if she chooses."

But before I had a chance to hear more about the matter, the murderous ambush by General Santa Anna's soldiers on the banks of the Río Bravo separated me for good from Bernardo's band. By the merest of chances, I escaped with my life. Whether any of the outlaws survived I cannot say. I raced north as fast as my horse could take me, but my erstwhile companions may have gone to Hell or Purgatory even more swiftly.

Slapping the Sultan

Lest he loll about as a veritable prisoner in his closely guarded palace, prevented by fawning officers and servants from seeing the true state of affairs in old Damascus, Sultan Hasan ibn Al-Rashad would often disguise himself as a common subject and with certain trusted officials following at a distance wander about the city at night to inspect streets and facilities for cleanliness or need of repair, observe the conduct of his night patrols, and be alert to criminal and immoral acts.

Late one evening not far from the palace itself and long past the time when honest subjects, to say nothing of decent women, had quit the streets and retired to their abodes, the disguised Sultan spotted a pretty, well-dressed Jewish girl hurrying along a thoroughfare at the late hour. By appearance and dress she did not appear to be a prostitute or thief, the only class of women one could expect to see abroad at night in Damascus. For the Sultan enforced a curfew and strict laws against unlawful and immoral behavior.

The Sultan was curious about the girl and ordered his officials to fall back and remain out sight as he accosted her to assess her character and learn her reason for being in the street at such a late hour.

He overtook the girl and asked to walk along with her, but to his surprise she responded to his suggestive offer with an indignant refusal.

"Come, come, girl," he said. "There is no reason for you to try to put on decent airs with me. For you must be a low-class woman of the evening looking for clients and sinful adventures. Otherwise, you would be indoors like all decent women."

Imagine the Sultan's astonishment when the girl turned and gave him a ringing slap to the face. His chief officer witnessed the unthinkable offense and ran to defend the sovereign and arrest the girl as she hurried away.

"Sire, her effrontery is beyond insolence! To touch the person of the great sovereign and dare aggress against him in such a violent and unholy manner is to earn the penalty of death! We shall bind the Jewess, as by her raiment we assume she is, and at first light put her to death!"

"Easy, easy, good captain, let us not be overly hasty," the Sultan said to the enraged officer, "but instead overtake her and bring her to me. The girl has shown that she may be worthy of our favor. Did she not act to defend her virtue against a man who accosted her, not knowing who I am? That does not seem to be the act of an immoral woman."

The terrified girl was brought back and ordered to kneel at the Sultan's feet. There she fearfully explained in reply to his questions that she worked as a housekeeper each day to support her widowed, ailing mother, and since her labors often extended into the evening hours, on those occasions she was obliged to walk home alone after dark.

Upon learning her name and more of the conditions of her life and family, the Sultan gently bade her rise, extolling her character and devotion to her sick mother, and ordering his men to escort her safely home.

"I would speak further with you, young woman. Present yourself accordingly in the imperial court on the morrow. There we shall make a determination regarding your circumstances."

The next day, after first making further inquiries into her family history and lineage, the Sultan assigned a generous pension to the girl, and after her mother passed from this life not long afterwards, saw to it that she was married to a proper and respected husband of her faith.

Thus, the slap, which would have been a death sentence in other circumstances and under other rulers, resulted in a vast improvement in the virtuous girl's fate under the enlightened reign of Sultan Hasan.

The Proper Level

In its callous way, fate often tests wise men, whether king or commoner, by giving them foolish children. For nothing separates men truly wise in all seasons and situations from others whose wisdom wilts when confronted with the folly of their offspring. Such was the case of Sultan Hasan ibn Al-Rashad whose youngest son Prince Jafar reeled from one disastrous decision to another in his early youth, proving thereby to be as vagrant in behavior as his father was firm in wisdom. But to add a good word about the lad, he behaved so recklessly not from malicious motives but from an utter lack of guile. This feature of his character led him to rely on the unreliable, believe the unbelievable, and trust in the treacherous.

On the other hand, Sultan Hasan coupled wisdom with patience, and since he loved all his children, he was determined not to let the weakest suffer more than his older offspring. To do so would be to add confirmation of ineptitude to his youngest son's notorious series of failures. Accordingly, the great ruler assigned the most accomplished and learned masters in his caliphate to teach Prince Jafar the secrets of science, the teachings of philosophy, and the principles of statesmanship.

"You were born a prince and it is your destiny to rule," he told Jafar. "And it will be your humiliation as a man if you prove to be unfit for this high calling. Had it been your fate to be a shepherd, then your moral duty would have been to be the best shepherd you could be. You cannot avoid the destiny fate places in your pathway, my son. So, strive with all your heart and mind to be the master of men and not the object of their deception and scorn."

Prince Jafar applied himself with renewed determination, for his greatest desire was to please his father. He listened eagerly to the alchemists and mathematicians, but he could see no purpose in their vile chemicals or find meaning in their complex numerical systems. He tried to follow the subtle dialectic of the philosophers, but he was quickly lost in their mental mazes. As for statesmanship, he could not understand diplomatic nuances. To him being a successful ruler was a simple matter of having greater armies than one's enemy, not bigger lies.

In the end, his teachers shook their heads and as tactfully as they could, informed the Sultan that Prince Jafar's exceptional talents did not readily lend themselves to scholarship and intellectual mastery. "Like your majesty, Prince Jafar seems to have a prior knowledge of all we present to him. Therefore, we respectfully submit that we can teach him very little and recommend in consequence that inasmuch as you are his best guide and model, you yourself, sire, can best instruct him in the high purposes to which he was born."

Sultan Hasan took no offense from the veiled insinuations that the young prince was limited in his understanding. Nevertheless, he silently agreed with the scholarly men that it was up to him to tutor the prince. But he realized that he must do so in more practical ways than the scholars knew. Indeed, he was already thinking of an alternate form of instruction for his son.

Accordingly, the next morning he summoned Prince Jafar to court and announced to the surprise of the assembly and the consternation of the older brothers, that he was appointing Jafar ruler of a prosperous Anatolian seacoast city east of the Bosporus. Jafar thanked his father and assured him that he would rule justly and by the wisdom of his decrees increase the prosperity of the already thriving city.

But no sooner had Prince Jafar installed himself in the city than it was stricken by a plague that killed nearly half of its subjects. Jafar was befuddled by the sudden calamity, and at a loss over what measures to take, withdrew with his retinue to nearby mountains as the panicked populace followed his example by also fleeing the city.

Jafar returned sorrowfully to his father's court with his dismal report.

"Did you examine the city's drinking water?" his father asked.

"No, sir, but what does drinking water have to do with the plague?"

"Mayhap a great deal, my son. The alchemists teach, as you perhaps recall, that impurities in the water may deposit poisonous impurities in the body, just as impure ideas corrupt the human soul. It is always prudent to proceed wisely in times of crisis. That way of a good ruler is to remain firm and calm, not dash hither and yon like a brainless chicken. Do you understand, my son?"

"Yes, father, for I know you would proceed as you say. I shall not make that mistake again. But, sire, what am I to do now? The city you gave me is deserted."

"I have decided to make you overlord of a smaller city closer to Damascus. It is well known for its lush grazing lands and excellent sheep herds. But you must beware the wild Kurds that lurk in the mountains to the north. Be vigilant against their trickery. They are bold and clever and would like nothing better than to seize our best herds. And see that the drinking water for herds and people remains clean and undefiled, lest a similar calamity occur as in the first city. Do you understand, my son?"

"Yes, father. I shall be diligent in all these matters and promise not to repeat my former mistakes."

Thus forewarned by experience and his father's words, Prince Jafar made his way to his new city. He found the herds fat and productive in wool and meat. The city well and nearby spring seemed clear of impurities. He then assigned guards to protect the water sources and soldiers to alert him to Kurdish incursions,

For a month all went well. Then one day, one of his captains reported that a Kurdish delegation bearing gifts had requested an audience with Prince Jafar.

"Tell them to approach unarmed, and under truce I shall hear what they have to say. But have our men at the ready. My father tells me that the Kurds are clever and bold."

The Kurdish chieftains approached unarmed as requested, and behind them servants carried gold rings and bracelets, silver broches and pendants, perfumes, silks, and other valuables.

"Hail, great Prince, son of our mighty Sultan," the paramount chief greeted him, "we come in homage and peace."

"You are welcome guests in this city provided you abide by my father's decrees. Accept our hospitality and thanks for the fine gifts you have brought us."

"They are but a modest earnest of the Kurdish tribe's intention to be good friends and neighbors. We are aware that in the past we Kurds have not always enjoyed that desirable description, in great part because our enemies have slandered our good name, but also because our ancestors did not always conform to the standards of respectful peace and solid friendship. The failure on our part we pray you allow us, their modern descendants, to remedy, great ruler."

"And how do you propose, esteemed chieftain, to establish a

relationship of peace and friendship between your tribe and this city?"

"If it please you, noble Prince, I propose to you a truce activated and enforced by a formal treaty signed by you or your emissary and my humble person, as paramount chief of the Kurdish tribe."

"We shall consider the matter," said the Prince, "but first let us celebrate these tentative steps with a banquet. You are our guests under our protection and subject to our hospitality."

Jafar was pleased indeed with the idea of making peace with the troublesome Kurds. Perhaps, he thought to himself, my father will come to see that I have developed the diplomatic skills I lacked before.

In due course the truce was signed and stamped with official seals and accompanying pledges of undying friendship. Then the happy, well-fed Kurds returned to their mountain fastness, leading as a gift from Jafar a dozen of the city's finest and fattest sheep. Then he informed his guards and soldiers that they could relax somewhat the close, tedious watch over the city's water suppy and prize herds.

"The Kurds are now our friends and allies," he explained to his skeptical lieutenants. "They will not break a formal truce to which the paramount chieftain has given his word and affixed his signature. To do so would be a personal disgrace that would besmirch his reputation as the brave leader of his people. The Kurds have been strong enemies of my father's caliphate; now they will be our strong friends."

And so they were—for a month. But on the night of the next full moon the Kurds swooped down in force from the mountains, and before the sleeping soldiers could mobilize to repel them, the raiders ordered their Christian slaves to pollute the city well and sheep spring with swine carcasses. Then they slaughtered the weakest sheep and made off with the best of the herd. When the city dwellers discovered the disaster, they cursed Jafar's ancestors and hoped that Sultan Hasan himself might burn in hell for assigning such an inept governor. They had no choice but to abandon the city, for no follower of the Prophet (blessings be on his beard) could drink from wells contaminated by swine blood. In their mountain fastness the Kurds celebrated their ruse and ridiculed Jafar, who returned in great sorrow to his father.

"Father, I have failed you again," he said, hanging his head. "I am nothing now in your eyes. Would that I had never been born, for I am thorn in your side, a worthless son, a blight on your greatness. Punish me as you must and send me into farthest exile so that sight of me will not annoy you."

"Easy, Jafar. It is ill in the sight of God for you to berate yourself so. Remember that you are his creation. I was given the care of you in this world and so call you my son because of it, but He is your Creator, and you must respect his creation. Yes, by the report your lieutenant gave me, you failed because you trusted in the promise of a scoundrel whose word, written or spoken, is as worthless as a bird dropping. Yet you failed in a single task, not in the multitude of acts and decisions that make a life. Now you must take on a third task. You have learned from your first failures. For your own sake, see that you do not fail in this one."

"As you direct me, father, so shall I obey. What is your will for me?"

"Long before our family was elevated to honor and power and indeed before the Prophet himself came into the world, our forefathers dwelt in the city of Samarra near the great river Tigris.

Destiny favored our line and with patience and labor they accumulated wealth and property from whence grew in time the power we now hold. Our family long held sway in the city, but the last survivor of our line there has, I learn, passed from this world, and his offspring have preceded him in death. There, son, you will bend your steps and rebuild our family heritage. And by doing so, you will increase the prosperity of the city, now ravaged and diminished by wars and the shifting tides of fate. How you do so is something you must decide. Only this advice will I give you: in all your dealings, be honest and astute, forgetting not the lessons of your experience, though they be contrary to your nature. And treat all men as you would be treated, honoring them in a way that honors you."

Jafar was grateful for another opportunity to prove himself and worked diligently to restore Samarra to its ancient standing. He built good roads to the Tigris River landing, restored the docking facilities, and built caravanserais to encourage traders and merchants along the trade routes to rest and take their repose in the city. In time new merchants came to set up shops. Craftsmen, carpenters, hostelers, and money changers followed. In ten years Samarra had become a thriving crossroads of prosperity under Jafar's enlightened governance. It was then that he was summoned to Sultan Hasan's court.

"What have I done that disappoints my father?" he asked himself, worried that he had made yet another blunder.

After a joyous reunion with his father and a cordial reception by his envious brothers, Jafar apprehensively asked the reason for the summons.

"I have decided that you must leave your present position as governor of Samarra," he told Jafar.

"Your will is my command, honored father, but may I respectfully ask what has so displeased you in my time as governor that you must remove me a third time from my position?"

"You must not assume, my son, that every change of position is a consequence of mistakes you have made. On the contrary, I am pleased to learn from my ministers that you have restored Samarra to its former status and made it a center of profitable and honest commerce."

"Sire, to the best of my modest abilities, such has been my aim since you named me as its governor ten years ago. But now I learn that I shall be reassigned. How and where may I serve you?"

"Henceforth, my son, you shall be the ruler of Baghdad with plenipotentiary power to issues decrees and enforce my imperial law and will over the city and its territories. Such has always been my plan for you."

Jafar could scarcely believe the good news he was hearing. Before he bethought himself to curb his tongue, he blurted: "But, sire, if from the beginning you intended me to be the ruler of Baghdad, why did you first send me to small provincial cities? Why did you not appoint me as ruler of Baghdad from the start?"

"Because you were not ready for your destiny and in one form or another would have brought the same calamity to Baghdad that you caused by inexperience and poor judgment in the coastal city and sheepherding town. In Samarra you have shown that now you are ready to rule. It was a matter of elevating you by stages to the proper level."

The Power of Resurrection

Not many years after the enlightened Sultan Hasan ibn Al-Rashad (blessings be on his head) passed from this world into Paradise after a long and glorious reign and his son Jafar the Wise ably ruled the caliphate in his stead, Abdul, a young Bedouin shepherd of obscure lineage but uncommon ambition, left his grandfather's tent and sheepfold near Al Qa-rah in the Hamad region of the Arabian desert and set out for Baghdad in search of enlightenment. Although his grandsire was loath to see Abdul go and tried his best to dissuade him, fearing he would encounter dangers far greater than those he had faced as a young shepherd, he gave him his blessing and all the food and water Abdul could carry.

"I have not gifts to bestow on you, my son. By the decree of fate and the will of Allah, we are a poor people on whom fortune has not smiled, and poorer still since death claimed your father before his time. But because I give you these meager items with great love, may they serve you in ways we cannot foresee. And may Allah grant that before these old eyes close for the last time, they may behold once again your beloved countenance."

Although Abdul listened patiently and respectfully to his grandfather's words, he was eager to be off in search of a special kind of knowledge. Since earliest youth his imagination was set aflame by stories he had heard of the Prophet Isa (Jesus) of whom it was said he could cure any illness and even raise the dead to life. Surely, Abdul reasoned, Prophet Isa knew magic words and incantations that enabled him to raise the dead to life. The great masters of knowledge, he thought, must have retained knowledge of these secret words of power or mayhap possessed talismans invested with such miraculous properties. His ultimate hope, if he discovered the secret of resurrection was to restore his father to life. So completely did his desire for the power over life and death consume him and drive from his thoughts concerns for his welfare that by the time he reached Baghdad he was reduced to begging for scraps of food for his stomach, and his garments had frayed into rags.

Despite his wretched appearance and thin facial hair, for he was still years shy of a full manly beard, in his ignorance of protocol, he approached a powerful Imam passing through the Bazaar with his disciples and without preamble revealed to him the object of his quest. Whereupon the famed Koranic scholar and teacher called Abdul an ass-brained fool and ordered him to quit his presence at once, lest he order his disciples to beat him for his impudence. The bewildered Abdul fled as the Imam's followers hurled refuse at his head and heaped insults on his father and ancestors, accusing them of being adherents of the hated sect of Isa, or if worse were possible, heretical Sufis, or even diabolical Zoroastrians.

Abdul dared not linger in Baghdad, for word of him quickly spread and he feared that the Imam's followers would espy him and fulfill their master's threat. Thus, dejected, his very life at risk, and without further hope in Baghdad, he wandered into the desert with a water bag and a dry crust as his only links to life. After trudging aimlessly for three days, he saw ahead of him a bent figure walking in the same direction, but burdened by the weight of many years, moving at a much slower pace. As Abdul drew abreast, the gray-bearded elder sank down on a rock, sighing as though about to fall into mortal expiration. Then turning toward Abdul, he extended a claw-like hand in supplication and said barely above a whisper:

"Youth, I famish to the point of death, give me a morsel that I may live."

"Sir," Abdul replied, "I have eaten the last of a bare crust and am myself now without food, else I would share willingly with you."

"Shall I perish in the presence of one so generous with nothing? Have you water, that at least I may drink?"

"Sir, I have only a residue remaining in this water bag, and it is all that stands between me and death."

"How? What perversity is this? I have before me one who would share generously the abundance of what he lacks, but selfishly withholds what he possesses!"

Stung by the elder's words, Abdul unloosed the water bag from his waist and gave it to him. The elder eagerly seized it and drank until it was almost empty. Then, as Abdul looked on in despair, he poured the remainder at the root of a wilting yellow vine at the base of the rock where he sat.

"By all that is holy, sir, why did you not save the last drops for me instead of pouring them on this vine?"

"You gave me to drink because I have a voice to request it. This vine was likewise thirsty but being mute could not ask. You must grow in mercy and understanding of all living beings if you would find what you seek."

"But, sir, I have not told you what I seek."

"The desires of the simpleminded are written on their face."

"Know you, sir, the object of my search?"

"I know many things, though they are but drops in the infinite ocean of creation. Now I must continue my journey. As for you, remain here and search inward and you may be granted the power you seek."

"But, sir, here there are only bare rocks and barren desert. Without food and now without water, I shall surely perish in this wasteland."

"That may be, but if fate has decreed your death, you will die the same and as soon elsewhere as here. Every mortal being spends its life trying not to die but consumes itself in the effort of living; and everything lifeless aspires to life with similar struggles. This vine had the same fears for its life and death as you when this day dawned. Now see how it flourishes."

To his amazement, Abdul saw that the elderly sage was right. The vine was now curling its tentacles around the boulder and its leaves shimmered with vivid gold and yellow hues. He turned to express his surprise, but to his even greater astonishment, the elder had vanished.

He was famished and thirsty. Perhaps I can at least find some shelter among the rocks, he thought, but can I survive night prowlers and desert cold without blanket or shelter? And what shall be my chances tomorrow? Stealing carefully between the great boulders in the deepening twilight, he suddenly came upon a cave entrance where a moment earlier there appeared to be only solid rock. He peered in cautiously, fearful that it might be the lair of carnivorous beasts. He saw and heard none, but as he entered and made his way deeper into the cave, he became aware of a peculiar luminescence, which without apparent source grew brighter the further he went in the confusing labyrinth of openings and tunnels. Then weak from hunger but comforted by the relative warmth of the cave, he lay down under a sheltering ledge and soon fell into a fitful, dream-filled sleep.

A terrifying roar woke him, and he shook with dread that bloodthirsty beasts were about to devour him. But instead of animals, he saw that the odd luminescence was gathering and swirling into a form before him. In an instant a gigantic translucent figure towering far above the cave, yet somehow still within its dimensions, spoke with a voice like thunder:

"Who dares enter my sanctuary? Stand forth that I may regard you!"

"I am Abdul, o great one," he said, coming from under ledge and shaking with fear. "I came this way seeking enlightenment, but I must have food and water or else I perish."

"I see that you are a mere mortal. I knew your kind in ages past when I was abroad in the world, and the memories are not pleasant. Yours is a pestiferous tribe, and I care naught for your needs. It is I who need nourishment. Procure it for me and I may spare you."

"I beg you for mercy, oh great one. But I must tell you in sorrow that I am without food, and the sage who accompanied me for a brief time drank all my water."

"All?"

"All but a few drops that he poured on a vine near the entrance."

"Bring me fruit from the vine and I will spare you."

"But, mighty one, there is no fruit, only a small vine in its first growth. And though it seems to grow swiftly, a season must pass before it can yield fruit."

"Mortal, since I was imprisoned in this cave ages ago, I have not tasted food or enjoyed other pleasures I once knew. Unlike your puny race, my kind cannot die, though our being may shrink, but my hunger and solitude have grown greater than I can bear. Bring me the fruit of the vine and I shall grant you a wish. Fail and I shall destroy you in my wrath."

"And if the vine has no fruit, what then, mighty one?"

"Then neither shall you have life and I shall be doomed to remain here as the ages roll on. But go and bring me fruit and all will go well for you if it goes better for me."

Abdul went out without hope of finding ripe fruit, if indeed the vine had survived at all. But great was his astonishment when he saw it grown to the size and strength of a rope and draped as far as he could see over boulders and sagging with golden fruit of a kind he had never seen before. The succulent juice at once quenched his own thirst and restored his failing strength. He gathered as much fruit as he could carry and returned in triumph to the cave.

As the gigantic being devoured the fruit its form and features became more clearly delineated and tangible but proportioned in ways so terrifying that Abdul could not look upon them, least of all its eyes, which blazed like crimson torches.

"Ah, how good to savor once more the golden fruit we knew in Earth's youth before the curse destroyed so much and spared so little. Now for a season I am restored to myself. But in my exuberance of being, I weary of your troubling presence, mortal. Yet to rid myself of you, I shall keep my promise. What would you ask of me?"

"Great one, I desire the gift of healing, even the power to revive the dead and restore them to life, as Prophet Isa did in his time."

"Ah, Isa, the great Lord of the supernal host to whose matchless power even we genies must bow in submission. His hosts broke the power of the titans and chained them in hell, and for our own misdeeds imprisoned us for eons in these dark, deserted places. But these matters far outreach your understanding. Therefore, mortal, go raise the dead, play the fool, and suffer the consequences! For you tamper with forces far beyond your control and understanding."

The genie laughed, a laughter that shook the cave with reverberating echoes. Then everything seemed to rotate, slowly at first, then faster and faster until Abdul could focus neither sight nor sense on anything around him but was afloat on nothingness for an immeasurable time.

He came to his senses beside a deserted cemetery of untended tombs and broken headstones overgrown with bramble and thorny shrubs. He did not recognize the place and could not read the strange names etched on the stones. But it mattered little to him: regardless of who the people were, here they slept the long sleep of death, and he had come to recall them to life and the light of human happiness. He fell to his knees and touched his head to the ground in the manner the elders had taught him to pray. Then rising, he extended his arms heavenward and ordered all in the cemetery to rise from the earth and live again.

At first there was no movement, and all was still. Perhaps the Genie deceived me, he said, thinking himself an utter fool. Then the ground began to shake, slightly at first then with increasing force. A grave opened, and slowly an old man clambered out, trailing tatters of burial linens and exuding an awful odor of decay. Then another tomb yielded its occupant, this time a young woman of fair countenance no doubt snatched by death in the flower of her life. Then other graves burst open and newly undead persons of diverse ages and conditions emerged. Even though he could not overcome completely his fear of the dead,

Abdul was beside himself with joy. He had the long-sought secret power, and his mind raced with visions of raising not only his beloved father but also hordes of deceased persons to their former station and condition. There was no limit to the good he could do. Or so he thought in his innocence.

But then the earth convulsed violently, deep crevices opened in the cemetery, and primitive trees and monstrous animals emerged, first as shadowy images then as solid forms. Seeing the hapless resurrected humans, the beasts pounced on them with hideous roars, ripping claws, and tearing fangs. Although they tried to escape, their shriveled legs were no match for beasts resurrected from earth's primeval ages. Soon all suffered death a second time and more violently than the first. Abdul sadly acknowledged his tragic mistake.

"I should have asked only for the power to restore humans to life, not every creature or plant that lived here in the dawn of time."

He resolved to find his way back to the genie to amend his request. But it was no easy task to find the cave. Eventually, he made his way back to Baghdad and from there retraced as best he remembered his journey into the desert. After several days and once again with only a half skin of water and two pieces of bread, he recognized the bent figure of the elderly sage trudging slowly ahead of him.

"How? You again?" he said as Abdul overtook him. "Why do you tempt fate by returning here? What do you seek this time? Were you not granted your petition?"

"Indeed, sir, but in my thoughtlessness, I asked too much and caused great suffering and destruction. Now I come seeking less than I was granted."

"Great power can be controlled only by great beings; the weak it will destroy," he said, seating himself on the rock. "Do you understand now that you must learn to use the powers you have, not ask for those beyond your abilities?"

"But, sir, my intentions are pure. I wish only to serve Allah."

"Have a care in claiming purity of intention for yourself. It requires great enlightenment to know oneself. And know that the best way to serve the All-Sufficient One is to serve the deficient sons and daughters of men. But I weary and thirst. Have you water to share with me?"

"Sir, as before I have a little in this water bag, and it is yours," Abdul replied, handing him the bag.

"You are learning," said the elder, taking a sip and returning the rest to Abdul.

"Sir, will you not water the vine as you did before? See how it droops, and its fruit, lately so rich and succulent, has fallen to the ground, soured and rotten."

"The vine must learn to care for itself. Before it asked for water, now it begs. Beware of repeated charity; extended too often, it creates sloth and defective character."

"Your thoughts are hard to follow, sir. No sooner do I understand a truth than you present an opposing one."

"You are learning, but do not rush understanding. Hasty knowledge is the greatest enemy of wisdom."

"The genie of the cave helped me when I brought him fruit from this vine. I fear that without it, he may not open his cave to me or grant my request."

"Perhaps yes, perhaps no; the human world and its matters teeter ever on a balance to favor our schemes or dash our dreams. Yet if there are many alternatives before us, there is always only one possibility behind us. You may in time learn the meaning of what I tell you. But for now, I must continue my journey and you must again seek entrance to the cave."

Abdul looked up, distracted by a rustle in the dry vine leaves, and when he turned again to speak to the elderly sage, the old man had vanished. Then with growing anxiety he searched among the fallen fruit for edible specimens and finding only three he took them to the spot where, as best he remembered, the cave entrance had once opened to him. Again, it was open, and with equal portions of relief and dread, he entered.

"So, mortal," the genie's voice echoed in the labyrinth of shafts and tunnels, "you trifle with fate by returning to defile my abode with your unsightly presence. What seek you this time?"

"I come with a twain of requests, great being: first, that you would accept this fruit of the vine in which you took delight before, and second, that you would reduce the power you granted me."

"Give me the fruit and I shall first consume it, though it appears overripe. Then I shall consider your second request."

As the genie devoured the fruit, it appeared to become more corporeal, though less substantial than the first time. Afterward it was silent for what to Abdul seemed to be several hours. But he dared not disrupt the silence. Finally, there was unseen movement and the Genie spoke:

"Now, mortal, what is this new folly you speak of, more power when you cannot control that which you were given?"

"No, mighty being, the power you granted me was too great and caused calamity and pain. Restrict, I pray, the power to return the dead to life to humans only."

"So it shall be, mortal, if only because I would see the outcome of this strange petition. For since the world began human creatures have craved ever more power, never less. What new folly is afoot among them now?"

The genie laughed uproariously and as the hilarity echoed down the corridors, again the cave seemed to rotate, slowly at first, then faster and faster until all was a blur and Abdul lost all sense of direction and time. When he came to his senses he was standing on a mountainous ledge overlooking a gleaming white city spread out on one side along a broad river and flanked on the other by orchards and fertile grain fields.

Abdul descended from the mountain and entered the prosperous city, marveling at its handsomely arrayed inhabitants and ornate structures. Then he slaked his thirst at a bubbling public fountain and, after inquiring of strangers, found his way to the spacious city cemetery. How happy these prosperous people will be to have their loved ones restored to them, he thought, for death seems to be their only enemy amid so much prosperity and good fortune. With this thought foremost, he prayed and commanded the dead to rise.

Like a disorganized host, the dead came forth from their tombs, many in fine array, many old, many young, many frightened, many delighted, but most dazed, and not a few bewildered by the sudden interruption.

But not long after the undead marched away to their former families and abodes about the city, many came back to the cemetery pursued by angry mobs as cries of terror and sounds of violence arose throughout the city.

"Why was I rudely plucked from Paradise and brought back to suffer again the infirmity of which I died in torture? Curses on the demons that caused this misery!" screamed one distraught and angry woman.

"My wife poisoned me and married her lover. Now they pursue me to murder me anew after I was safely dead!" cried another.

"My sons and heirs revile me for fear that they shall have to forfeit the fortune I left them! They will not let me enter my own house! What am I to do?" moaned a dejected man.

"Two years after my death my faithful husband took another wife and happiness returned to his house. But now that I have reappeared, she accuses him of duplicity and returns to her father's house, vowing never to sleep again under her husband's roof," lamented a woman.

"I lived to extreme old age burdened with all the ills that excessive years bring. Death was a welcome relief. No fate could be worse than resuming my old agonies. More life in such decrepitude is a punishment I do not deserve," complained an elderly man too frail to walk.

"I was a despised beggar in this world," wailed an aged woman. "How can I live again in this vale of tears and misery after knowing the bliss and beauty of Paradise?"

Seeing the terrible effects of his misjudgment, Abdul vowed to return once more to the genie to beg that the power to resurrect the dead be stripped entirely from him. Perhaps then, he thought, I may return to my Grandfather's tent and flocks to live a normal life and die in the proper way when my time is over.

So it was that he trod the desolate way to the Genie's cave, and as he now expected, once more overtook the elderly sage.

"How? You again! You wax ever bolder in your encounters with the Genie. But have a care; it is not wise, and may prove dangerous, to tax his patience."

"I promise, esteemed sage, that this shall be my last visit to this place."

"Have you then satisfied your desires and conceived no new ones?"

"Better, I think, o wise teacher; I have thrust them out of mind, and I shall ask the Genie to remove them from my spirit entirely, if he will admit me once more."

"Have you water for me?"

"I bring a skin full and half of another. Drink as you will and water the vine if it please you."

"I am not thirsty. The water is for you."

"Esteemed teacher, I see that the vine is dead. How shall I entice the Genie to receive me if there is no fruit?"

"The vine lived and died, and in so doing, fulfilled its destiny. Do not look to the dead to resolve the problems of the living."

"I do not understand."

"I weary of hearing you repeat these words of bafflement. You do not understand because you do not yet understand yourself. Cast aside false dependency and proceed henceforth as one who walks without crutch."

"I shall do my best, sir."

"No, you must do better than your best. For what you thought to be your best has proven to be your worst, has it not?"

"Indeed, it has," Abdul admitted sadly. "Then will you, respected master, show me the better way?"

"No, we shall leave that to the Genie. Therefore, approach the cave and if he is willing, he may teach you a bit."

Abdul turned to obey, then bethought himself and looked back to thank the sage, but again, as before, the latter had vanished. The cave entrance was open for him, but the luminescence was gone, and all was darkness when Abdul peered in. The only sound was the dripping of water somewhere in the recesses. He waited in the darkness until finally a voice spoke:

"Step forward into the light."

He took a tentative step, fearful of stumbling and falling. Suddenly the cave was brilliantly illuminated by a light that seemed to come at once from nowhere yet everywhere. Then as his eyes adjusted to the brightness, he received his greatest surprise. For there before him reared not the fearsome Genie but stood instead the elderly sage, though not bent and weak as he was in the light of outer day but erect and stalwart as one in ageless strength.

"You!" Abdul blurted in astonishment. "But, sir, where is the Genie?"

"I am the Genie and the Genie is I. We are both but neither entire."

"Though it displease you to hear me say it again, great master, I do not understand."

"Ignorance sometimes grows into wisdom. Perhaps that will be your destiny."

"Willing would I learn at your feet, Master, but first I beg you—as Genie or Master—to take from me the power to resurrect the dead. Once I thought it a blessing for good but now see it as curse for evil."

"Consider it done, Abdul, and know that it was never a real power you possessed, but an illusion cast over you to teach you the folly and peril of aspiring to powers beyond your ken and control. Only the greatest celestial masters can control such mighty powers as you desired. For their own good, mortal men must stay within the limits of their mortality."

"What then should I do, great master, that ignorance and its folly may not rule and ruin my life?"

"Begin with what is right and honorable: return to your Grandfather's tent and flocks and serve him with love and obedience all the days of his life. And when his days in this world have ended, we shall see where destiny next leads you."

"Revered Master, will you be there to guide me when that time comes?"

"Fret not about time and circumstance, nor think to prolong the present after its day has passed. When the student is ready, the master will appear. For masters are many in the flesh and diverse in their methods, yet one in spirit."

Abdul obeyed the sage, and when his grandfather passed from this life old and full of years, he bartered away his inherited flocks and left to study under a great master in Baghdad. Whether it was the same sage he knew in his youth, the chronicle does not tell. All that we know of his later life is that Abdul waxed great in wisdom, left many descendants, and was remembered for many generations for his enlightened teachings and charitable acts.

The Flightless Bird

By chance an egg fell from an eagle's aerie and landing on soft leaves and moss, rolled uncracked into the ground-level nest of a flightless bird. Although the egg was larger than the others, the mother bird nudged it next to her own and sat faithfully on all until they hatched out as normal wingless chicks. All that is except the oversized eaglet. And as mothers will, the wingless mother bird loved her strange chick and defended it against her rude neighbors who poked fun at its unnaturally large wings, long hooked beak, grotesque feet, and clumsy way of walking and scratching for worms and grubs.

"What a shame and embarrassment for the whole ground bird community," clucked the oldest biddy.

"Indeed," squawked another. "She or someone should have taken the freakish creature into the forest and left it there for foxes or serpents to devour."

"Aye" cackled a third, "but the poor mother is blind to its birth defects that are as plain to the rest of us as the beak on your head."

"Mother," the eaglet said to her one day, "I have a strange feeling that I should fly. Can you teach me?"

Oh, what next for my poor baby? she thought. Fly, indeed! It's hard enough teaching him to scratch for grubs with those deformed feet of his. Soon he must go out on his own. Then what will he do? How will he live when I can no longer care for him? For I shall have other eggs to hatch and new broods to care for.

"Son," she said with sincere love and concern, "put such foolish thoughts out of your head! Flying indeed! What an outlandish idea. We live on the ground like sensible birds. Here is where our food is, not up in the empty sky. We are what we are, and that is the way we must live, as we always have, here on the ground."

"But, Mother, I see things that look like birds flying through the air. What about them?"

"They are strange birds. Why they soar and swoop about in the empty sky, always at risk of falling, is beyond me. No sensible bird would be so foolhardy. Be thankful, son, that we are not like them. Our place is here on the ground where all reasonable creatures live. Be happy that we are what we are. We were not meant to fly but to walk on solid ground."

The very idea," she thought to herself as she scratched more vigorously to relieve the frustration she felt with her strange son.

One day a majestic eagle flew down and perched on a nearby treetop. Then peering down at what appeared to him to be a little eagle, he asked if it was old enough to fly.

"Oh no, sir. My mother tells me that we are ground birds and that our kind cannot fly."

"But you look like a young eagle to me, and eagles fly. It is our way. Are you sure you cannot fly?"

"Quite sure, sir, though sometimes I have the odd desire to try. Life is hard for me. For unhappily, as you can see, I was born with several defects that limit my abilities and make it hard for me to find food."

"But I see that you have long, well developed wings."

"Yes, but sadly they are a nuisance, always getting snagged in the underbrush and making it hard for me to snatch bugs."

"Your talons seem to be almost developed enough to seize prey."

"I know nothing about what you say. What I do know is that curled as they are, it is hard for me to scratch for grubs."

"Your beak is developing a handsome curve and will soon be strong enough to tear prey into edible chunks of meat."

"But it is very little help in grabbing the mites, grubs, and worms we eat. The only good it does me is to give strong pecks to those in my community who poke fun at me. My mother has to warn me at times not to pluck out their feathers."

"So, even though you look like an eagle, walk like an eagle, and have wings, talons, and a beak like an eagle, you insist that you are a flightless ground bird?

"Yes, sir. It is my destiny."

"Have you ever spread your wings and tried to fly?"

"Oh no, sir. We are ground birds."

"But have you ever thought that you might be another kind of bird, a flying bird?"

"Once or twice I dreamed of flying, but my mother told me to put the idea out of my mind."

"And did you?

"Yes, sir."

"Why?"

"Because my mother always tells me the truth."

"She told you her truth, but have you ever wondered what your truth is?"

"Is there a difference?"

"Perhaps, but you will never know unless you search for it."

"But all my life my mother and my community have told me that we are ground birds."

"And so you have been, or have acted as such, but your destiny could be to soar in the heavens like me and eat real meat, not spend your life scratching for measly worms and grubs in the dirt."

"Even if I could learn to fly off into the sky, I would be afraid to try."

"I will help you if you are willing to try. For you have the features of an eagle, none that resemble the traits of flightless ground birds. I shall fly back this way tomorrow to see if you are ready to try your wings."

The eagle flew away, and the fledgling considered his offer of help. But the next day when the eagle flew back to the treetop, the little one was still too afraid to try. And the next, the same; and so, too, the next; and the next. Finally, the great eagle flew away for good, and as time passed, the little eagle forgot his dream of flying.

"I am a ground bird," he said as he scratched clumsily in the dirt for worms. "I can only be what I was born to be."

First Blood

On the morning of April 17, 1775, a fisherman saw Susan Pickford's corpse floating seaward in the Charles River. Her body was fully clothed, but her dress was torn and there were bloody lacerations and gashes on the face and head. Constable Albert Stanley reported it as a probable homicide and the murderer most likely a thief surprised in the act of burglarizing the mansion.

"What about the officer quartered in the residence? Have you questioned him for relevant information?" asked his sergeant Milton Blackmore.

"Sir, you should know that Lieutenant John Beaufort-Essex, though of questionable morals, so I am told, is nonetheless a British officer from one of England's noblest families. I thought it best to avoid antagonisms with the British militia under the tense circumstances of the moment, and to take special care not to impugn his illustrious family."

"Yes, yes, wisely done," the sergeant replied. "But in the interest of justice, we must at least get a statement from him. We are within our rights to do so in a matter this serious. What about servants and maids and Mr. Henry Pickford himself?"

"Sir, Mr. Henry Pickford is insensible with grief, and despite its size, the residence at present employs only two servants, an elderly cook of Scottish extraction, Nattie Mckenzie, and Miss Pickford's maid, Mary South, in age near to her mistress. A gardener was terminated two months ago and has not yet been replaced. Mr. Pickford is said to be meticulous in his selection of servants. The cook claims to have heard nothing, having retired early and slept soundly. As for the maid, she is beside herself with grief and unable as yet to give us a credible account of what she may have witnessed or overheard."

"What do we know about the Pickford girl's normal activities and habits?"

"Sir, the neighbors describe her as a model of discretion and decorum, that she is—or was—betrothed to a young man by name Jeremy Atwater of the Lexington Township, and that her wedding was set for June."

"Aha, now we have information that may yield us results," the Sergeant said in a more forceful tone. "Love is mother to many tragedies. For where love is, jealousy stands beside it as its image and shadow, stirring hatreds and shaping devilish misdeeds, including murder. Bring that fellow to me at once! He bears careful questioning, and I shall do that myself!"

"Yes sir, and what should I do about Lieutenant Beaufort?"

"For the moment nothing. Fetch me the girl's lover, and when the maid has recovered her tranquility, we shall question her."

Jeremy Atwater broke down in despair at the news of Susan Pickford's death, sobbing and cradling his head in his arms. When he had regained a measure of self-restraint, he looked up at the sergeant with tears in his eyes and rage in his voice.

"Sir, you must arrest that damnable Redcoat quartered in Master Pickford's house! He's the guilty one! He's to blame!"

"Have a care with reckless talk, my good fellow. Your grief is understandable, but baseless accusations will get us nowhere. Why do you point a finger at Lieutenant Beaufort-Essex, Mr. ah . . . Atwater?"

"Because I know that he is responsible for my sweet Susan's death. That's why."

"And how do you know?"

"Because Susan told me."

"Jeremy, is it? To put the matter in plain words, Jeremy, Miss Pickford is deceased and can tell us nothing. Explain yourself."

"Sir, she told me not above a week ago that the Lieutenant had spoken to her in language that disrespected her modesty and bordered on lewd suggestion. Ask the maid; she will tell you the same, I am sure."

Later, the maid denied any knowledge of what Atwater claimed.

"Were you not Miss Pickford's personal maid and privy to her affairs?" the Sergeant asked her.

"Yes sir, I'll not deny it for truth's sake. But Miss Susan told me little of this matter. I know nothing about any of this."

"Let me tell you this, Miss South, we have a suspicious death on our hands, probably murder, though as yet not officially declared as such. If you should by an unwise decision conceal information from city authority, which I represent in this instance, you may be guilty of complicity in a crime."

The girl's blue eyes, big and round, showed her fear. "What means complicity, sir?"

"Complicity in a crime means sharing the guilt for it. We do not assume that you had to do with Miss Pickford's death. Indeed, as I said, we do not know officially that she was murdered. That is why we are asking questions of all who knew her. But if her death was a criminal act and you keep anything you know from us, then it would mean that you could be to some degree guilty yourself."

"Oh, merciful God! Then I shall tell you all I know and withhold nothing. I loved Miss Pickford and kept her daily in my prayers. And I miss her terribly. She was so good and kind to me, and likewise to one and all."

"Did she have enemies, people who disliked her or with whom she had problems?"

"Oh, no sir, she becharmed all, young and old, men and women alike. She was a saintly girl, kind and good to everyone."

"Tell me about her betrothed, Mr. Jeremy Atwater."

"A kinder gentleman never lived, sir, and none could match him in devotion to Miss Pickford. Miss Pickford told me that when they yet resided in the Lexington Township, Mr. Atwater was but a lad, yet already he saw in Miss Pickford his one and only love. In those early days he worked for Mr. Pickford in the making of apple cider, hauling the mill from one farm to another in the country thereabouts. Then being of age and with a wish to establish himself in a livelihood when Mr. Pickford retired to Boston, Mr. Atwater arranged to buy the mill on generous credit terms offered by his old master. In this way, their friendship remained lively and in the case of Miss Pickford blossomed into a hearty wish to unite their lives and fortunes in marriage. They were to wed in June. Oh . . . how the thought of it doth grieve me now!"

"What can you tell me about Lieutenant Beaufort, lately quartered in the Pickford home?"

"Oh, sir, that is a harder task you ask of me."

"Why so?"

"Because so as not to be guilty of—what did you call it, 'complication'?"

"Complicity, Mary, complicity; so, you must tell me what you know, no matter how unpleasant it may be. Did Miss Pickford confide in you about the Lieutenant's attentions?"

"Yes, sir, I must confess that she did, but the matter was not so simple as a gentleman's improper regard for a young lady."

"You must explain that remark. Tell me the whole of it in your own words, Mary."

"Yes, sir. Well, I know not whether the regard the Lieutenant had for Miss Pickford was an expression of honest sentiment. It was said that, though young in years, he was old in . . . worldly experience. That I cannot speak to. For all I know, it could have been the idle chatter of servant girls. But what is certain is that he was dashingly handsome."

"Mary, this sounds like the first page of a bookish romance, but what has it to do with Miss Pickford?"

"Their conversation, so she confided to me, advanced to talk of matrimony."

"But was not Miss Pickford already affianced to Mr. Atwater at the time?"

"Indeed, sir, and that was one cause of a great conflict in her sentiments. The other was that she was unsure of the Lieutenant's sincerity. Her father told her that in olden times in England the Pickfords were attached to the Beaufort manor as workers and servants, but problems arose and the Pickfords left England and resettled here. Miss Pickford confided to me that she was not altogether persuaded that Lieutenant Beaufort was not pursuing some twisted plan of revenge on her family. Besides, she loved Mr. Atwater with a settled love nearly as old as they were. And she remembered fondly her young years in the country. But now she was older and educated in the best Boston schools. As she said, country life was a pleasant memory, but her life was now very different. The more she thought about it, the less sure she was that she could go happily back to the country and the old ways. The Lieutenant was a fresh, exciting emotion and the pathway to a life beyond her grandest dreams. Or, as she first feared, a nightmare of scandal and deception. Miss Pickford put it this way: Jeremy was the happy past; Lieutenant Beaufort was the promise of a greater future. Jeremy Atwater was a man of farms and forests, plain, decent, and devoted, whilst Lieutenant Beaufort was a man of the greater world, clever, of high aristocratic class, and dashingly handsome."

"Are you telling me that Miss Pickford intended to break her engagement to Atwater and transfer her affections to the Lieutenant?"

"Sir, she was sorely tempted, so she told me privately, and at the last yielded to his suit. Her sentiments for the Lieutenant had grown so great that they pushed aside all other doubts and uncertainties."

"Did she tell Atwater of her decision?"

"Sir, unhappily, she did, her sense of loyalty to Mr. Atwater demanded it, she insisted. For she was straightforward in all things."

"Unhappily, you say. I take that to mean Atwater took the news badly. Did he?"

"Sir, I cannot speak directly to the question, for I did not speak again to Miss Pickford about it."

"When did their conversation take place?"

"Rather late in the evening before her death."

"And you did not see her afterwards, that is, after they had talked?"

"No sir, it was late, and I was in my room and likely abed before he left the house."

"Was the Lieutenant in the house at the time?"

"No sir, I think not, but I have no certain knowledge of his whereabouts that evening. That same day it was gossiped about that the Redcoats were about to begin a military action of some kind."

"Yes, so we have all heard. Mary, is there anything else you have neglected to tell me that might have to do with Miss Pickford's death?"

"Oh, no sir! I swear on my mother's grave that I have told you all I know about the sad matter. Please do not think I am guilty of complica—complicity. I am an honest girl."

"So you are, Mary, so you are, and I am convinced of your truthfulness. You may go, but as the matter progresses, you may be called on to repeat what you have told me."

After she left, Blackmore summoned Constable Stanley to his office.

"Stanley, if the Pickford girl's death was a murder, pending the coroner's inquest, then we have our criminal. Bring in the man Jeremy Atwater."

"You think he is responsible in some way for her death, not the Lieutenant?"

"I do indeed. As for Lieutenant Beaufort-Essex, a man of his standing would never offer an honest proposal of marriage to a girl of her class. In my judgment, the proposal that the servant girl Mary South reported was simply a ploy to bed Miss Pickford. And the circumstances of the case and what Mary South told me lead me to believe that he succeeded in his purpose."

"How so, sir? I do not understand your reasoning in the matter."

"Mary South told me that Susan Pickford was exceptionally straightforward in all she did and said. I take that to mean that she was somewhat limited in her thinking and too rigid in her understanding to be aware that for safety's sake the truth must be shaded, softened, or silenced in certain circumstances. If she had simply told Atwater that she intended to break her engagement because she loved another man, he would have suffered and protested, but eventually accepted it. But if she rashly admitted to him that she had already given herself to his rival, he would take it as a betrayal that would so lower her in his sight that he would not scruple to act in jealous rage. I have learned in this business that nothing is so protective as pure love, but nothing so murderous as pure jealousy."

"What do we do about Lieutenant Beaufort-Essex? If this is murder, as it surely seems to be, does he bear any guilt?"

"I am afraid only a moral guilt. Lieutenant Beaufort is by all accounts a rogue and a philanderer of the first rank. But those same qualities would mean that he had no reason to kill the girl. If she resisted him today, he would turn his attention to another woman tomorrow. His feelings appear to be of the shallowest kind. Atwater, on the other hand, is a simpler but deeper man who once he gives his heart to a woman can never commit to another. His very steadfast devotion is his downfall, just as the Lieutenant's shallowness is his exoneration. As a formality we shall ask Lieutenant Beaufort-Essex for a declaration when his company returns from its maneuvers, but I am thinking at this moment that Atwater may be hanged for a crime of passion."

*****

But events that transcended the death of Susan Pickford, yet were connected to it, prevented any contact Constable Blackmore intended to have with Atwater and the Lieutenant.

On April 18, 1775 Lieutenant Colonel Francis Smith dispatched a force of seven hundred soldiers to Concord to seize and destroy a rebel arms cache. An irregular company of some seventy-seven Massachusetts militia intercepted them at Lexington but were under orders to withhold their fire. Nevertheless, a shot was fired, and a skirmish ensued that left eight militiamen dead and one British officer wounded, a certain Lieutenant John Beaufort-Essex.

After considerable casualties, the reinforced British forces fought their way back to Boston where they were under siege for nearly a year, by which time military matters greatly overshadowed civil law and the majority of Bostonians no longer thought of themselves as Englishmen but as Americans.

"Who fired on the Redcoats?" asked the annoyed rebel leader. "We had agreed to hold our fire. It does not help our cause for Englishmen to kill other Englishmen."

"Sir, it was the cider man Jeremy Atwater well known in these parts. He lies dead yonder under the maple tree. He was the first to fall."

"I like not to speak ill of the dead, but hotheads like him will set this land ablaze with war. His shot will echo far and wide, and who can say to what outcome?"

"Sir, he fired at the commanding lieutenant, then dropped his musket and ran, arms outstretched, towards the Redcoat line as though seeking death. At least a dozen balls struck him, but when we dragged him back in a moment of truce the Redcoats allowed us, he still lived, though barely, and he spoke words with his dying breath."

"A madman, no doubt. What did he say?"

"Nothing that made sense to us, sir. As best we could

understand, his last words were, 'I have no right to live and every reason to die. Dear God, forgive me my unforgivable deed.'"

*****

Lieutenant John Beaufort-Essex served honorably throughout the Revolutionary war. For though a man of flawed morals, there was never any doubt about his valor. Ironically, he was unscathed in several major battles but limped all his life from a wound received in the first minor skirmish of a war destined to change the world.

Milady's Trunk

Part I

In its usual careless way, fate decreed that in May of 1671 Sir Henry Beaufort-DuCordier, 72, should arrive widowed, exhausted, and all but penniless in Hampton of the Virginia Colony with blonde, beautiful daughter Katherine Elizabeth, 19, and his only remaining servant Matthew Tyler, 23, at a time when Richard Blackwell, 31, was consolidating a fortune from land, lumber, cattle, and shipping enterprises. With a purse much weightier than his pedigree, Blackwell dismissed Old World class differences with New World brashness, and with his characteristic boldness wasted no time in asking Sir Henry for Katherine's hand in marriage.

The prospect of his daughter marrying below her class duly troubled Sir Henry, but aware of his approaching mortality he desired above all else to leave Katherine materially well situated. The possibilities of doing so were few. An old Yorkshire friend and comrade in arms, himself newly established in Hampton, had promised Sir Henry help but died shortly before his arrival. The man's family, fearful of offending the colonial authorities and dreading unwelcome requests for aid from the impoverished old aristocrat, shunned him as though he were a biblical leper. In these straitened circumstances Sir Henry reasoned that a union with commoner Blackwell not only would assure Katherine's future but also might restore in his last days some of the comforts the family enjoyed before the Cromwell debacle. He had entertained similar hopes when his older daughter Madelaine-

Marie married her distant cousin Baron Roger-Antoine DuCordier. But this hope was quickly dashed. The Baron was fractious in his emotions and miserly with his purse. Sir Henry grieved over the fate of Madelaine-Marie but was powerless to remedy the state into which she was now sunk. Thus beset with misgivings and praying that circumstances would not repeat themselves in the case of his younger daughter, he gave his consent and ordered Katherine to prepare herself to become Richard's bride.

But unbeknownst to Sir Henry, Katherine had other hopes. With even more swiftness than Blackwell, Phillip Sterling, 25, adventurer, soldier, singer, and favorite with the plantation gentry, had won her heart with his seductive songs, erotic good looks, and eloquent pleas of true and eternal love. Possessing nothing, he was free to promise her everything.

A war of wills commenced between father and daughter and battle lines were drawn. Sir Henry claimed the traditional paternal right to marry his daughter to a man of his choosing, even to a commoner. Katherine protested that she loved another—Phillip, if he had to know, yes, Phillip Sterling—and that no father in these modern times had the right to overrule a woman's heart with antiquated Old-World customs.

"Heart! Heart! 'Od's blood! What hath heart to do with the matter at hand?" Sir Henry thundered in his antique speech. "Will thy strutting jack-a-dandy provide thee roof and warmth with his magical song and verse? Will his poetical fauncies and capering daunces feed thee when thou hungerest? Or clothe thee decently according to thy estate? Tis commonly bandied in this towne that Sterling is an idle runabout who giveth no thought to the morrow and maketh no provision for leaner days. Sweet

Katherine, well do I know his kind; heedless of life's common demaunds, in a trice would hee traipse away to new adventures, leaving thee shivering in want and neglect. No, I say, by the Saviour's Blood, no! Darling Katherine, thou canst take to husband no such man! Thou, the apple of mine eye, the light of my old age, by God's grace must have a better provision. My days of mortal life are but in few numbered, and it were a double wound of death to pass from this life without leaving thee conveniently wedded to a provident husband. Though thou mayest forget all else I tell thee, sweet Katherine, remember well these words: long after the springtime of young love hath passed and the poetry and song are but fading echoes, the harsh demaunds of this cruel world will abide to trample underfoot the rootless fauncies that beguile thy reason. No, No, dear Katherine, I say a thousand times no, I cannot give thee in marriage to a man who lacketh the manly will and material wherewithal to provide thee a pleasant living. Think with thy head, sweet daughter, rein in thy riotous heart, and thou wilt see the wisdom and fatherly affection that govern my intentions for thee."

Eventually, after many tears and screams of protest Katherine grudgingly realized that her aged father was right. The ruination of her family in the Royalist cause and their privations amongst miserly relatives in France and indifferent acquaintances in the Virginia Colony were painful lessons she had not forgotten. And despite her feigned aristocratic aloofness in material matters, she had inherited determination and foresight, ancestral traits that in earlier ages had won the Beauforts, DuCordiers, Montagues, and Montgomerys lands and noble titles in England, France, and Wales. Thus, despite her strong-willed character, in the end Katherine could not bring herself to trample her father's will. She loved Sir Henry dearly and her respect for him had grown all the greater as she watched him stand unbowed as his fortunes crumbled, his wife and sons died, and feckless friends turned their back on him. He lived by the chivalric code of olden times, a man whose word was sacred and dishonor worse than death. Sir Henry was magnanimous in victory and undaunted in defeat. When all was said and done, Katherine could not bring herself to add further burdens to Sir Henry's misfortunes. She made her decision: her heart ached for Phillip, but her head ruled otherwise. She would marry Richard but only under two conditions: first, that he provide Sir Henry a decent residence and, second, that although she would live under his roof, until she might decide otherwise, their union was to be a formal bond without physical consummation. Richard generously complied with the first but objected energetically to the second.

"It shall be as I have said, or it shall not be at all," she stated in an unmistakable tone of finality. "I remind you, sir, that it is you, not I, who seek this marriage."

"Very well, Miss Beaufort, but I shall nourish the hope that in time our marriage will grow into a deeper union."

"I promise nothing, sir, beyond what I have said."

She kept her word and married Blackwell in January of 1672, sending most of her remaining possessions to his mansion in a great trunk inherited from her French *grand-mère*, Marie-Angélique DuCordier, and to which she alone had a key.

Looking to provide for his faithful servant Matthew Tyler, Sir Henry requested, and Richard granted, that upon the old aristocrat's decease the Welshman would serve in their household, even though Katherine had never really warmed to Tyler, who, she feared, knew too many of her secrets to be trusted.

But just as Sir Henry invoked Old World paternal authority to marry her to Richard, so Katherine, reflecting formative years spent among her DuCordier relatives in France, privately claimed the unwritten French right of a woman in a loveless *mariage de convenance* to compensatory liberties, including, should she so choose, an occasional discreet indiscretion. Her loyalty to Sir Henry was unbreakable, but her fidelity to Richard, beyond her stated conditions, was unsworn and untested. Her head would rule and she would wed Blackwell, but her unbridled heart would reserve its right to private subversions.

If Katherine was secretive in her movements and sentiments, Richard was perceptive in his. He had not become one of the richest and most powerful men in the Virginia Colony by allowing others—men and women—to outwit him. He trusted no man fully and women not at all, for he proclaimed as an unarguable fact that by nature the fair sex was susceptible to beguilement and seduction.

Thus began a cat and mouse game between them. Richard was angrily aware that his young bride did not love him and for that reason was all the more determined that at least she would not dupe him. For her part, Katherine was equally committed to guarding her womanly prerogatives and keeping at arm's length a man who to her was more a stranger than a spouse. From the first, mutual distrust and suspicion distanced them and prevented any sort of intimacy. William removed into the east wing of his mansion from which he ran his enterprises and orchestrated espionage of his wife, leaving the more finely appointed west wing to Katherine, her maids, and her intrigues.

Soon after their wedding and almost coincident with Sir Henry's demise, rumors began reaching Richard's ears that servants had seen Phillip Sterling prowling about the estate. Alarmed and angry, Richard ordered increased vigil over the grounds, but despite these precautions, Matthew Tyler, now elevated to majordomo of the household with the passing of Sir Henry, claimed to have seen Sterling, or someone resembling him, running from the west wing of the mansion early on a December morning. Richard readily believed what he quickly suspected and flew into a jealous rage, swearing openly to kill his rival should he discover him trespassing on his property. Weeks passed during which Matthew reported more rumors of Sterling's nocturnal prowling. But try as he might, Richard and his men could discover neither hard proof nor circumstantial evidence of his wife's infidelity. And because he lacked firm evidence, he could make no credible accusation against her. But the less he knew the more he imagined. Their relationship, confined to meals, church, and social events, was tense but formally correct.

One morning Matthew hurried to Master Blackwell with the disturbing news that an hour before daybreak guards had seen a man leap from a window above the rose garden. But before servants could detain him, the intruder disappeared, as best they could tell in the foggy gloom, perhaps into the west wing of the mansion itself. They searched but found nobody.

"You have searched everywhere?" asked the angry Richard.

"Yes, sir, everywhere except . . ." responded Matthew, hanging his head.

"Except where? Regard me, man, when I am speaking to you!"

"Sir, everywhere except Milady's room. Naturally we dared not go into her chamber but summoned her maids instead to enter therein."

"And what did they find?"

"Sir, they reported no trace of an intruder but instead found Milady staring silently at her locked trunk. She was not her usual talkative self, so they said, and responded not a word to their inquiries. They described her as fully dressed for the day but with eyes red from weeping."

Richard muttered an oath under his breath. Then, his mind in turmoil with inflammatory images, he ran to her bedroom, taking only enough time to arm himself with a pistol and saber.

"Madam," he asked as calmly as he could manage, "what is the matter here?"

"Nothing is the matter here, Mr. Blackwell, though from the voices and noise I hear, there appears to be commotion outside. See to it, sir, and leave me in peace. I am not ready to receive anyone."

"Mayhap you have already received a person, Madam," he said, glancing at closets and bed coverings. Seeing nothing untoward, he approached the trunk with drawn pistol and rapped it with the handle.

"Your actions and insinuations belittle you and offend me. Sir, explain yourself."

"I believe it is you, Madam, who owe me an explanation. Tell me, what is in this trunk?"

"What the trunk contains is my affair. But if you must know, as surely you do, it holds my personal belongings."

"Then you will not object to opening it in my presence?"

"Indeed, I object, sir, and most strongly, for your words cast doubt on my honesty."

"By opening it and verifying the truth of your words, madam, you could easily allay any doubts I might have."

"Your doubts would be laid to rest only for the moment. Matthew would soon poison your mind anew and manipulate your thoughts and actions with more gossip. Allow me to point out clearly what is at stake here for you, Mr. Blackwell. If I open the trunk and it reveals only my belongings, as I have truthfully declared, then you, sir, will be exposed for the fool you are hard bent on becoming. Regardless of any orders we might give them to keep silent about the matter, servants would gossip, as servants always do, word would spread, and you, sir, would be the laughingstock of Hampton. On the other hand, should you discover, as you seem to suspect, that it conceals a lover, it would prove to the whole world that you are a miserable cuckold, deceived in your own house and under your very nose. Everyone in Hampton would then scorn and mock you. No, Mr. Blackwell, out of respect for you and this household I will not open the trunk. You may open it yourself, if you choose to do so, but be prepared for the belittling consequences of your act. And if you wish to speak to me further of this or any other matter, sir, hereafter I shall be at the residence my father left me."

With that she summoned Rose, her African maid, to pack her personal items in a silk satchel, removed a heavy brass key from an *étui* and tossed it contemptuously on the floor, and, with head high and young Rose following in matching posture, marched haughtily from the room.

Richard bent to retrieve the heavy key and moved to open the trunk. But then he stopped and thought for several minutes, tapping the key in the palm of his hand. Suddenly he pocketed it and stepped outside the room to call Matthew.

"Yes, sir?"

"Hie you to the dock and fetch Captain Bradford. And tell

him to bring six stout men with him."

"Yes, sir, at once."

Captain Bradford appeared within the hour.

"Captain, I know that many matters claim your attention before you sail the *Bristol Maid* for Jamaica tomorrow. But the order I shall give you now stands above all others. Have your sailors rope this trunk tightly and carry it aboard the vessel. On pain of flogging—hear me well—on pain of flogging, if not death itself, for any man who would dare disobey my orders, now become yours, do not open it under any circumstances, regardless of any sounds issuing from it during the transport. Should the sailors query you about the trunk and its contents, tell them only that you act under my direct orders and order them in the strongest voice to stay a distance from it. Keep it under your personal vigilance until you are well out to sea beyond sight of land. Then order the ship's carpenter to weight it heavily for sinking and heave it overboard. And never speak to me again of this trunk. Is that clearly understood, Captain?"

"Perfectly, sir, it shall be done as you order. But as Captain, may I be privy to its offending contents?"

"The contents are not your concern, Captain, but mine alone. Kindly follow my orders and query me no further."

"Of course, sir, they shall be carried out to the letter."

"Then see to it. That is all. Good day to you, Captain."

Captain Bradford's men staggered under inordinate weight of the trunk. Blackwell made no comment, but inwardly he was convinced that Sterling—a strapping muscular man—must indeed be locked in the trunk. Excellent, excellent, he thought to himself, reasoning that if Sterling drowned in the trunk and the body should by happenstance be discovered, then, if queried, he would say that his wife told him it contained only personal items and that he ordered it to be disposed of at sea consequent to disputes it had occasioned in their marriage. In which case, the guilt would shift to her. And if she should confess that Sterling was indeed sealed inside, then her lie and the fact that only she could unlock the trunk from the outside would both destroy her reputation and absolve Richard of all but the mildest degree of culpability. Such was the jealous ire her behavior had aroused in him.

When Katherine learned from the servants what Richard had done with her trunk and how he had dealt with his dilemma she shook her head and sighed. Tears came to her eyes as she realized fully for the first time the dangerous game she had been playing. "Oh God, why did I let the matter play out to this gruesome end? But there was no other way except to do as Phillip instructed me. To do otherwise would have been to risk having him discovered in my room to the ruination of my reputation and his probable death. Had Richard discovered him, he would have killed him without ado with a pistol ball to the head. There was no other way, no other way," she whispered to herself several times. "Now that my sweet Phillip is gone. Oh, *mon Dieu*, my God, how shall I live without him? How, how, dear God? But I have only myself to blame. I chose my lot and must forever silence the truth of it. Now my life must be with Richard and all other feelings must be set aside. But oh, dear God, to think that I shall never see sweet Phillip again! Never! Never again! But my loveless life must go on, bleak and bitter as it is."

Despite her despondency, she was stunned by the astuteness with which Richard resolved the seemingly irresolvable dilemma of the trunk, thus placing the onus squarely on her. He is more cunning than I thought, she whispered to herself. I underestimated him. No wonder he has amassed power and fortune. Her grudging admiration of Richard weakened her loathing of him but without replacing it with warmer feelings. Nevertheless, it was a prelude to a rapprochement of sorts, and she admitted to herself that prudence, if not love, must oblige her to suffer the dreaded consummation of their marriage.

Within the week she took the first step toward ending her estrangement by returning to Richard's house. But her return was not peaceful; the first two nights, loud, angry disputes and accusations of the most intimate matters issued from her bedroom to the scandalous entertainment and gossip of the eavesdropping maids. Then, abruptly, on the third eve, the quarrels subsided and the next morning the maids discovered that Master Richard and Lady Katherine had slept in the same bed.

Soon thereafter Richard sternly rebuked Matthew Tyler for what he described as the "bootless accusations" that had so agitated Madam Blackwell. Nevertheless, despite increasingly severe tongue lashings he kept Tyler in his service and position until 1679, when in a violent rage he ordered him flogged and expelled from his estate.

Thinking the matter of the trunk resolved in this draconian manner, Katherine and Richard did not speak of it again and unable to foresee a better life, reconciled themselves to a marriage rooted more in truce than troth.

But the resolution was soon reopened to questions. Three days after Captain Bradford sailed for Jamaica, a powerful storm, plowing its way up the American coast, battered Hampton, tearing roofs from houses, flooding the lowlands, uprooting trees, and raising Richard's fears that it had swamped the *Bristol Maid*. Indeed, later evidence confirmed that the vessel was lost and likely all aboard perished in the storm. Seamen arriving from Charles Towne[1] some weeks later reported seeing a broken mast, torn sails, cables, spars, casks, and a portion of the *Bristol Maid* hull washed up on the outer Carolina banks. The remains of two corpses among the wreckage provided gruesome evidence of the disaster when a sailor identified one of the corpses as that of Captain Bradford.

The loss of the *Bristol Maid* aroused only abstract feelings of regret in Katherine. She barely knew Captain Bradford and the crewmen, for Richard chose to tell her little about his commercial affairs.

Blackwell soon recouped the loss of his vessel and cargo, but an unidentified assassin murdered him in 1679, leaving Katherine with two infants, Henry, 5, and Mary, 4. She assumed personal supervision of her husband's complicated affairs and with considerable skill and determination kept the enterprises solvent. Other, more personal matters, however, took an unexpected and less fortunate turn, as related in the following accounts.

---

[1] Founded in 1670, Charles Towne was named in honor of King Charles II. In 1680 the city was relocated to Oyster Point, its present site. In 1783 at the conclusion of the American Revolution its name was changed to Charleston.

Part II

With the benevolent wisdom that Providence often grants loving parents, Sir Henry Beaufort had warned his daughter Katherine about Phillip Sterling. Her father's unflattering portrait failed to persuade her, yet moved by powerful filial affection, Katherine overruled her passion for Phillip and forced herself to wed Richard Blackwell instead. But she could not deny herself love a second time after Richard was murdered in 1679, a crime that remained unsolved in the colonial archives, and Phillip, believed dead, reappeared months later in a manner soon to be told. At first Katherine had the troubling thought that Phillip had to do with Richard's murder, but when she asked him about it, he responded that even if he had decided to kill his rival he would have been within his rights.

"Was it not Blackwell's wish, indeed his intention, to take my life? Would I, then, have no right to defend myself against him?" he asked rhetorically and with a wave of his hand dismissed other questions.

Katherine convinced herself that even if his moral reasoning was flawed, Phillip could not be an accomplice to murder, much less guilty of it himself. With self-serving logic, she concluded that her feelings alone exonerated him of wrongdoing. Her heart would not mislead her into loving an assassin and thus no further proof of his innocence was needed.

If in practical matters Katherine was resourceful and levelheaded, in sentiment she inclined, as did her mother, to idealistic dreaminess, a consequence, according to Sir Henry, of shunning devotional books and reading instead frivolous stories of chivalric romance and other unedifying tales. Since girlhood she had been enchanted by the idealistic philosophy of French thinker Blaise Pascal and embraced wholeheartedly his premise that the heart has its reasons the head cannot understand. Had she not experienced the conflict in her own case in deciding whom to wed? In any case, she reasoned, when played out to its last consequences, love conquers all, and with equally invincible benevolence, forgives all. As it was told in her favorite stories, so it must needs happen in life.

The practical, stolid Hampton townspeople were a world removed from her overblown philosophic idealism and fanciful daydreams of idylls and chivalric romances. They still had misgivings about Sir Henry and his daughter, but these were mild compared to the gossip that swirled through Hampton when instead of withdrawing into genteel retirement, as widowhood and custom dictated and the townspeople expected, Katherine took personal control of Richard's enterprises. Thus, it was an annoyance though no surprise to her that several vestrymen from St. John Parish and prominent townsmen should pay her a visit. After polite and practiced expressions of sympathy for the family tragedy, they reached the point of their visit.

"Madam," said Church Senior Warden William Glover, "if, at the behest of these gentlemen, I may speak to you in terms as respectful in intention as they are forthright in meaning, it does not seem meet to church and town folk of Hampton, in whose representation we come, that as a highborn lady you should engage yourself in ordinary commerce. Our chief concern, madam, touches on the questionable moral integrity of the commercial community and the proper decorum regarding your ladyship. We fear both may be offended if you, a Christian lady of the nobility, should be exposed to the uncouth language and tawdry sentiments that commonly attend the worldly commerce of the ruder sort of men."

"I thank you for your concern, Warden Glover, gentlemen," Katherine responded, nodding to one and all but with a crimson blush of annoyance on her cheeks. "But in this matter, I had no other recourse except direct involvement in my late husband's commercial affairs."

"Madam Blackwell," asked land broker and planter George Bradmore, "did you consider offering his enterprises for purchase and entering into retirement as befits a gentlewoman of your station?"

"Indeed, I did so consider, Master Bradmore, but the offers I received were so meager as to seem closer to theft—you will pardon my blunt words, gentlemen—than to legitimate purchase of my properties."

Almost to a man the delegation registered in their facial grimaces their disapproval of her strong language. The exception was stout Bradmore whose florid face turned a cherry red. For had he not secretly orchestrated a scheme to take advantage of her supposed naïveté in matters of business and acquire her lucrative shipping interests and choicest lands for prices far below their fair market value?

"Why may I ask then, Madam Blackwell," Glover asked, "did you not seek the aid and counsel of knowledgeable and estimable men versed in these matters and who could have guided you along a proper course of action?"

"Warden Glover, during those trying days no one save a few kindhearted women of the community offered sympathy in my grief, and of course none could give me reliable business counsel. As you know, our family standing in this community was unsettled during my father's lifetime and remained no less strained after his passing. You, sir, well know that the Church withheld its permission for his remains to be buried in St. John's cemetery. It was Rector Palmer's decision to deny him not only the accustomed Church rites of burial but also the merest Christian blessing at his funeral. The decision was to an extreme distressing to me, and my father's mortal remains yet lie unblessed yonder in a small family plot set aside for that doleful purpose. Thankfully, there were no such misgivings about my late husband's religious standing, yet old grievances still existed that made the circumstances of his death doubly hard for me to bear."

"Madam, I was not invested with the office of Senior Warden of the Church when Sir Henry passed away," Glover said hurriedly. "Had I been so, be assured that I should have acted as forcefully, and correctly, as Christian charity urges on your family's behalf. But you must understand, as surely you do, that the Church could not give its blessing to the questionable religious doctrines Sir Henry was said to profess."

"Had anyone bothered to inquire, sir, it would have been clear to all that my father had long since ceased to entertain doctrines, if indeed ever he inclined to them, at odds with the teachings of our Mother Church. The mistaken judgment about his religion was a supposition founded, so I believe, on his old-fashioned manner of speaking and not on any degree of sympathy for the variant Quaker beliefs of which he was accused. His antiquated speech had a simpler origin. It still lingered in his youth amongst the nobility and higher gentry of Yorkshire where he was born. Nor indeed had it completely died away in my early girlhood there, for I well recall hearing elderly folk so speak. To sum the matter plainly, gentlemen, it had naught to do with my father's religious beliefs before or at the time of his death."

"I should be the last person to question the truth of what you say and the first to believe it, madam," Glover responded in a calmer voice. "And I do hope you will recall my actions on behalf of your family in the case of the late Mr. Blackwell's tragic passing, actions which I believe were in complete conformity with our Christian faith."

"Indeed, I do so recall them, and am grateful, sir, and shall continue to be so, for all you did."

"Madam, gentlemen, we busy ourselves with matters that though touching do skirt our main concern," magistrate Benjamin Thompson reminded them, visibly annoyed and impatient to get back to his pressing affairs. "More to the point, madam, are we to understand that it is your intention to continue oversight of the commercial affairs of your lamented late husband?"

"Only for a time, master Thompson, only for a time. Gentlemen, given the concerns you have raised touching on the singularity of my situation, no doubt you will be interested and mayhap relieved to know that I shall close out my affairs in Hampton and remove my family from the Virginia Colony altogether. This provided I receive a fair remuneration for the holdings and enterprises left me by my late husband."

The surprised men looked at one another. "We are taken aback to hear you are considering departure from Hampton, madam," Glover replied, trying but failing to mask his jubilance with a look of Christian compunction. "We had hoped you would remain amongst us, perhaps in a retired state as befitting one of your genteel—"

Spurred to alertness by the good news, Bradmore leaned forward in his creaking chair and interrupted him, "Madam, most assuredly a favorable arrangement can be made for the equitable sale of your properties. I, for one, unselfishly offer you my help and advice if departure from Hampton is your decision. Though, of course, we shall all be saddened by your leaving."

The dignified delegation left shortly thereafter, happily congratulating one another and eager to report the successful outcome of their mission. Bradmore chatted but little, silently calculating how he was to acquire the Blackwell properties for himself.

None knew that Phillip Sterling—yes, Phillip Sterling in the flesh—had persuaded Katherine to make this decision. With the same cunning he had used to outwit servants on the eve of Katherine's wedding day, gaining entry to her room for a last passionate embrace, so now he reappeared, materializing as silently as a ghost in the early morning hours of a chilly March night. Katherine awoke to find a hand over her mouth to stifle her screams. At first, she feared physical violation or robbery, but as she began to make out the man's features in the gloom the greater terror of confronting a ghost paralyzed her. But then he spoke in the seductive baritone voice of the man she had loved so deeply.

"Gentle, sweet Katherine, gentle now, my love," Phillip said softly. Then bending next to her ear, he whispered in French, a language they had often spoken to each other, "*C'est moi, chérie. Je suis revenu, vivant, pas un revenant* (It is I, darling, I have returned, a living person, not a ghost).

Katherine commenced to tremble uncontrollably in wonder and resurgent emotions. Could it really be Philip? It was impossible, but his deep baritone voice convinced her; it was Phillip, unmistakably Phillip, whom she thought to have lost forever, who now took his hand from her mouth and gathered her in his arms. Again, she felt the urge to cry out, not in terror but in orgiastic, resurrected love long stifled and thought forever buried. He smothered her words and questions with kisses both to silence and to arouse her, and she responded with a matching passion that quickly transported them altogether beyond the need of sensible words.

Their lovemaking lasted for hours.

And in the morning light long after he vanished as silently as he came, she remembered his kisses and relived his embrace, wondering if it was all a dream.

It was not; his return was real and repeated in several visits in the dead of night. Yet the rekindling of their love and his return to Hampton, even the practical matters of where he had taken residence and how he slipped in and out of the town unseen and without the barking of dogs were secrets he said should remain so for the moment at least. He promised to explain to her the mystery of the trunk and to clarify other puzzling matters. "Mere trifles," he said provisionally, but he gave no further thought to keeping his word once given. For him his deeds spoke for themselves without any need of explanatory details. He acted as it pleased him, which alone was reason and justification enough. He felt no urge to please others, much less to inform them of his methods.

Not that Katherine objected; silence and secrecy suited her at least as well. Only six months had passed since Richard's death and she knew better than to stir ugly gossip by curtailing her mourning and having her name publicly linked to her former suitor whose reputation was both celebrated and sullied by the infamous episode of the trunk. Now and then yielding to curiosity and temptation, Katherine asked him how he had escaped the sealed and locked trunk. But he laughed and repeated only his claim that no lock could deter him. At times she all but believed he possessed magical powers of the dark arts.

During respites in their passionate trysts it took but little effort on Phillip's part to persuade Katherine to leave Hampton for Charles Towne in the Carolina Colony. His descriptions of its balmy climate, abundant commercial opportunities, and lax official oversight in England's southernmost mainland colony alone would have been enough to sway her. But to these attractions he added others. There, he told her, they could live in unmolested happiness as man and wife and no doubt easily enrich themselves in thriving Charles Towne through trade with a deeper south. For Katherine there was another reason she kept to herself: she longed to put a healing distance between her and Richard's death, for which she felt a lingering guilt. She wondered also how Phillip knew so much about the Carolina colony, but of this curious matter she said nothing at the moment. There were many chapters in the life of this strange, fascinating man that she was content to ignore, at least for the moment, provided she be allowed to keep her own secrets. Her inner life was vast and wondrously turbulent in its fancies, but she suspected that his was even more complex in real deeds and adventures. She loved him with an unquenchable passion, and the more she adored him, the more her effervescent imagination found reasons to love him even more.

Within days, Bradmore presented an offer to purchase her town properties and outlying plantations. This time he eschewed intermediaries and acted under his own name, offering a price much elevated over the first. Hat in hand, he explained his situation to her.

"Madam, I shall not withhold from you that at the moment it is far from convenient for me to tender an offer for these properties. My monies, a right modest sum to begin with, I assure you, are in the greater portion invested co-jointly in London and cannot singly be withdrawn. This circumstance reduces my disposable funds to a precarious level. Yet I took to heart our recent discussion of your intentions and am willing because of it to risk extending myself in order to aid you in disencumbering yourself of your holdings."

Discounting George Bradmore's customary lies and duplicitous affairs, of which she and everyone in Hampton were well aware, Katherine perceived that in this case there was a solid kernel of truth in his declaration. The offer, though not as high as she wished, was substantial enough to entertain. Bradmore was miserly but not moronic; he knew that others also desired the prime plantations and holdings and would push past him if he dallied or tried to place an inferior bid before her. And foremost in his favor, he could pay in genuine Spanish dollars, not in the colonial paper scrip, which in lieu of English coin frequently circulated in the Colonies but was not always honored at face value and was not acceptable in all places. On Phillip's advice and with minor upward adjustments in her favor and upon receipt of a substantial earnest, she accepted Bradmore's offer.

Katherine demurred only when it came to her ship, the *Kingston Elizabeth*, which Richard had purchased in replacement of the star-crossed *Bristol Maid*. She would have need of it, she explained to Bradmore, to remove her family and household belongings to her new home in Charles Towne.

He assured her that there were passable wagon roads to the Carolina Colony, but Katherine rejoined that she refused to endure the hardships and dangers of a land passage, especially the infestations of mosquitoes in the marshes, beasts in the forests, and natives along the route who were only sporadically peaceful. "No, Master Bradmore," she said with finality, "my vessel will not be a part of the transaction."

The transfer of funds and deeds duly completed, servants dismissed, scant farewells exchanged, her furniture and other belongings secured on the lower decks of the vessel, it remained only for Phillip to make his public appearance in Hampton to climax the events. Astonishment, disbelief, and lurid insinuations on the part of the townspeople attended his return. Everyone asked questions, but no one had reliable information about where he had been and what had happened to him. And he offered only the most insubstantial answers. The man was a deep enigma, and for many of the townspeople he provoked in equal portions admiration and distrust. As for Katherine, she could not wait to fly away with her knight errant, as the old idylls described. For a time, all her dreams returned with the imaginary extravagances of her girlhood.

They sailed from Hampton on a June morning to fair weather and a calm sea. Katherine, who was superstitious about signs and omens, took it as a propitious beginning of their life together. Phillip was busy conferring with the captain about the ship and the winds and absentmindedly dismissed her romantic fantasies with a quick kiss on the cheek.

Henry and Mary were wildly excited by the voyage and Katherine was soon busy supervising them and answering their childish questions about swooping seagulls and playful dolphins that cavorted alongside the ship. Phillip was still a mere stranger to them, which caused them to cling all the more to their mother. Katherine hoped he would soon win their trust and affection, but in the short time since he first appeared publicly in Katherine's company, he had paid the children only scant attention. For her part, Mary was inexplicably afraid of Phillip and her mother could not persuade her to sit on his knee.

On the other hand, in an oblique way Phillip was protective of Katherine herself. In the brief time of his return to Hampton most of the townspeople had turned openly against Katherine, reviving and enlarging suspicions about her earlier relationship with Phillip and speculating about Richard's unsolved murder. Malicious gossips whispered that Phillip could have had something to do with Richard's death and that Katherine might have been an active or passive accomplice to the crime. And in the eternal way of gossip, what began as unfounded whisper quickly spread abroad as fact.

Phillip quickly put them off track by offering a reasonable but false account of his whereabouts at the time of Richard's murder and his reappearance in Hampton. Dispirited in the months following Katherine's marriage to Richard, he explained to them, he had sailed for England, arriving just in time to bury his aged mother and settle her small estate. Although only distant kin remained in Stafford—his father had died two years earlier—he decided to settle himself anew in his ancestral town and blot from memory his troubles in France and sentimental disappointments in America. As for exaggerated reports of youthful misdeeds in Stafford, time had so erased these calumnies from collective memory that even should they have had substance, it would have occurred to no one to activate legal proceedings against him. By chance he happened upon a sailor recently on shore leave in the Virginia Colony who told him of Richard Blackwell's murder. He saw a chance to resurrect his unrequited love for Katherine and returned to Hampton for that singular purpose. He described himself as the happiest and most fortunate man on earth. For rare is the man, he said gaily, who gets a second chance at the love of his life. He laughed uproariously when reminded of the episode of Katherine's trunk.

"In all likelihood I was either boarding a ship in Chesapeake Bay for Plymouth or already at sea when Blackwell—with due respect for the deceased—had his comical bout of lunacy with her trunk. I concede that he was an able man in commercial matters, but he understood women not a whit, being as unable to distinguish between a highborn lady and a serving girl, as a boorish plowman would see no degree of difference between an Arabian stallion and a decrepit nag. Know, also, that in my fighting days in France I learned secrets that allow me to slip about undetected when I wish, though I fear no man living in singular combat if such an encounter should befall, as indeed it has many times, ever to the mortal disadvantage of my adversaries. Be assured that I would never put a lady's good name at risk or cast doubts on my valor by such an unworthy ruse as Blackwell imagined. He failed by such childish follies to be a proper husband to Katherine. I intend to see that she has a happier life at my side."

In this way, he deflected criticism from himself and softened some of the suspicions about Katherine. Nevertheless, if the good folk of Hampton could tolerate Phillip's love for beautiful Katherine, they remained scandalized by her haste to suspend mourning for Richard and fly to the company and—if the gossips were right—the arms of her former suitor. In any case, the margins of forgiveness for the sexes were, as always, unequal: laxly cast for Phillip and his extravagant transgressions, narrowly drawn for Katherine and her lesser trespasses.

As if Katherine's improper behavior were not provocation enough, the outraged town folk lacked but little to froth at the mouth when word spread in Hampton that she intended to sail unwed in Phillip's shipboard company. Former Senior Warden William Glover and other Church worthies urged an appeal to colonial authorities in Williamsburg to thwart this immoral atrocity, but most of the pragmatic townspeople were content to let them depart, thus happily ridding Hampton of further scandal.

No one asked Katherine herself, but had they queried her about this crowning impropriety, she would have reminded them that no civil magistrate or ecclesiastical authority would be willing to marry them in Hampton or Williamsburg. Besides, she was anxious to depart and avert further disapproval. She counted her years in Virginia as wasted and unhappy, much unlike her former sentimental expectations for her life in the Colony and were brightened only by Phillip's advent and the births of precious little Henry and Mary.

Winds and skies held fair for most of the voyage, but high winds made it necessary for the ship to stand off shore for two days before the sea was calm enough for safe docking in Charles Towne harbor. Phillip hired drivers and high-wheeled oxen-drawn wains to transport Katherine's furniture and belongings to spacious lodgings in the better part of the growing town. She and the children gaily squabbled over their living arrangements.

She was anxious to bring into conformity to common decency her irregular relationship with Phillip as quickly and discreetly as it should be possible. In the meantime, to forestall gossip and repeat the unpleasantness suffered in Hampton, she asked Phillip to take lodging elsewhere.

"You understand my reasons, do you not, my darling?" she asked apologetically. "I am thinking of us as a family and should like to make a happier beginning in this town than I did in Hampton. There would be lingering gossip about us were we to live here unwed as man and wife. I must think of the children and our future happiness."

"Of course, of course, my dear. I understand perfectly. I shall take lodging at the inn only a few doors removed from here."

"But let us wed at the earliest possible moment, my love," she pleaded. "Time apart from you is torture for me. You know how much I adore you, do you not, my precious darling?"

"Indeed, yet no more than I love and adore you, dearest Katherine. But now that we are alone, and the children are abed, I must explain a few things to you, my dear, being foremost among them that I cannot marry you under the name Phillip Sterling."

"What are you saying? I don't understand."

"The matter will seem bizarre to you, my dear, but in essence it is simple. Sterling is not my surname. I took the name when I came to America, and on this wise: I fled France unjustly pursued as a fugitive by the King's officers. It seemed prudent to begin life in America as Phillip Sterling, a new name for a new life, in the unlikely but possible event that French authorities should extend their pursuit of me to the English Colonies."

"Then, pray, what is your real surname?"

"Phillip Stafford is my birth name, taken in olden times no doubt from the name of my ancestral village in England. It is an honorable surname, though not of high lineage as is your family. I am the descended from sturdy yeoman stock who have risen to middling means and standing, my dear, and it is the name under which I propose to marry you so that our union may have an honest and upright beginning. Mayhap I could live here unmolested as Phillip Sterling. Yet the son of a Duke I was forced to dispatch to the next world defending myself in a duel was the much beloved young nephew of the Queen's bastard brother. He deemed it murder and swore he would not rest until he had exacted vengeance. His family is the northern branch of the Trémont aristocracy. You will pardon my saying so, mindful of your excellent ancestry, my dear, but it is always murder when by accident or reason a commoner kills a nobleman. That, in sum, my dear, is why as an expedient precaution I took the name Phillip Sterling."

"Do the Duke's agents pursue you still and are there risks that yet imperil you so far from France?"

"I learned from friends in England that the Queen's brother has died and his nephew was banished to Quebec for crimes that would have merited execution for one of lesser birth. For the first time in many years I breathe easier, thankful to the Almighty that a nightmarish chapter of my life is at an end. Now at last I can be myself again and live my life under my birth name. Europe's old ways, which aggrieved us both, seem less forceful in this New World. And there is a simpler reason: I prefer my own name."

Katherine stared at Phillip for a moment before responding. Then taking both his hands in hers, she leaned close to him and said: "Then, Master Phillip Stafford, I shall love you as devotedly under this name as I have heartily loved you heretofore as Phillip Sterling. But I hope most earnestly that you have no more surprises to unnerve me further, as so many events have done in growing measure since Richard's death."

"None, my dear," he laughed. "Now you know all my secrets, as you are in full possession of all my love."

"Not all your secrets, my darling," she smiled. "There yet remains the mystery of your uncanny escape from the trunk and the way you came and went without detection in Hampton. At times I wonder if you are versed in devilish arts."

"Trifles, my dear, mere tricks and trifles that I shall explain to you in due time."

"Then we can be united in matrimony and live openly and happily as man and wife as we dreamed of in Hampton?"

"Indeed, my dear, indeed, and the sooner the better for me. Yet I must explain two other matters before we consummate our happiness."

"And what matters are those?" Katherine asked warily. Your words affright me."

"They are matters fraught with no little embarrassment to me, my dear."

"Confide in me, my love. You know you may trust me."

"Well do I know that, dear Katherine, and the comfort it gives me is beyond telling. Yet the certainty of your love makes it no easier to reveal these matters to you. Rather the contrary."

"I promise you all the succor that lies within my power to give."

"Very well, but I shall beg you to think no less of me."

"That goes without saying, dearest Phillip, so tell on. My curiosity grows apace with my nervous anxiety."

"Then hear me out before you respond. To begin with, I departed in haste from England, so great was my desire to see you again. Nor would I do things differently did I again face that pressing but happy prospect. In consequence, I took not the time to put my affairs in proper order, but rather disposed of my ancestral properties quickly without due regard to their true worth. My thoughts were centered on my love for you and practical matters suffered accordingly. A distant cousin took advantage of my eagerness and purchased them for a trifling sum."

Katherine opened her mouth to speak, but Phillip put a finger to his lips to silence her.

"As you may easily imagine, therefore, my assets, modest to begin with, melted away as I made my way back to America. For reasons I shall explain, I had hoped to reunite with two maternal uncles of mine living on the island of Barbados in the Antilles and to Bridgetown in that place intended to bend my steps. I remembered in particular the benevolence and largesse of my Uncle William Woolsey, younger of the two, and though my memories of Uncle Alexander were fainter, for he had left England earlier in life to seek his fortune in the Antilles, I do recall that he was no less pleasantly disposed towards me. Providence had favored both and it came to be said latterly in our town that from comfortable circumstances in England they had risen to riches in Barbados. Unhappily, for a number of reasons I was not able to go to Barbados."

"My love, could we not continue on to Barbados and make our home there? Your uncles are established men of substance and if both feature a kindly disposition towards you, surely they would welcome us as a family, would they not?"

"Indeed, my darling, kinder, more generous men are not to be had in all the English realms. But the problem is their age. After half a lifetime spent away from Mother England she now calls them homeward. They wish to return to our town there to live out their last years. My uncles are dear to me, but once they have departed the island, I should not wish to subject you and the children to the backward conditions of Barbados. Only a few English families of means and class reside there, so I am told, and lacking books and instruction even they have sunk nearly to the level of uncouth sailors and tradesmen, and, indeed, only a bare margin above illiterate plantation workers. Barbados is an isolated island far from civilizing European influences and populated in the main by indentured Scots, Irish, and English, most of whom are brutish in the extreme. Charles Towne may seem little better at the moment, but the arrival of more desirable English folk will soon transform it into a civilized city."

"But that—", Katherine started to say. Again, he put a finger to his lips to interrupt her.

"Allow me to conclude, my dear, for I must say on about what I intend to do in order to put an end to my lamentable state of near penury."

This time Katherine would not be silenced.

"You dear, dear man, there is no need to concern yourself with material matters. You have me, and I have estate and fortune aplenty for us both, enough for you, for me, the children, and more offspring if God so blesses us. For I confess I want nothing so much as to bear our child. Or children," she added as a crimson blush spread across her cheeks.

"Were our condition reversed, I should repeat your words with the same sentiments. For I share your high hopes for our family. But I am a man, my darling, and I cannot live on the largesse of a woman, not even the woman I love and intend to take to wife."

"You spoke of a plan, and if your heart is bent on fulfilling your manly aims, then explain them to me so that I may lend you my unstinting support in all possible ways. But understand well, my darling, that I deem those intentions needful only for your manly satisfaction, which I respect for your sake but do not urge because of any material want or desire on my part."

"Duly noted, my dear. The plan is this. There is a great shortage of building lumber in Barbados and neighboring islands where the tropical storms called hurricanes spawned off the African coasts are often especially destructive of buildings and human life. The native woods are soft and generally unfit for durable construction and, in any case, the best forests have been cut away for sugar and indigo plantations in all desirable sites, leaving only the stunted forest growth on mountain slopes. Very fine lumber may be had in Spanish, Dutch, and French dominions on the Southern Continent not greatly distant from Barbados, but the Spanish are arrogant and adversarial with the English, the Dutch greedy and deceptive, and the French corrupt and treacherous. The great cypress and pine forests of Carolina produce excellent lumber that will fetch a handsome sum in Barbados and other islands. And though this commerce alone will be lucrative, it may be doubled or tripled by merchandise transported back to Charles Towne."

"What sort of merchandise is that? Sugar, indigo, or tobacco?"

"Slaves, my love, African slaves. The commerce of indentured servants from British realms is less dependable than it was in former times, and whites are ill-fitted for labor in tropical lands.

Yet Barbados is the outermost of the Antilles and thus closest to the great African continent and the first port for the slave ships bringing their human cargo to the West Indies and the Americas. My plan is this: I shall, with your assent, hire crews to cut cypress lumber hereabouts in Carolina, then transport it along with sundry other goods—metal items particularly—on the *Kingston Elizabeth* to Bridgetown in Barbados. On the return voyage I shall bring a profitable cargo of slaves needful in Charles Towne and the plantations growing apace in the Carolina Colony."

"The vessel is yours, my love, for the purposes you describe and other uses that may arise later, but I confess it disturbs me greatly to hear it will be used to transport human chattel. Betimes I heard my father declaim against slavery, for in this particular he did indeed agree most cordially with the Quakers. More than I knew at the time, his opinions continue to have a compelling power over me, and even though I myself have owned servants, I treated them humanely and prefer not to think overmuch on the conditions under which they were brought to this land and came into my possession."

"Then if it causes you moral anguish, my love, we shall forego the slave trade altogether. There are other commercial ventures in the Antilles that I may undertake in its stead. But now I must present the second and most painful aspect of my proposed enterprise. I am without funds to put my plans into play for the reasons I revealed to you. And while I am pained beyond measure to say it, I find myself in the embarrassing circumstances of having to appeal to your generosity to give them a beginning. I am newly arrived here and men of substance in Charles Towne who could give me backing know me not, though one day they shall, indeed they shall."

"My darling, all I possess is yours. Dispose of my funds, our funds, as you will."

"My love, you are the woman of my dreams!"

"More than a dream, my hope is to be the only woman in your life."

"And that you are, my love, and that you shall always be."

Few days passed before Phillip contracted with slave owners to send logging crews into the forests to cut and haul the giant cypress logs to the Charles Towne wharves.

Meanwhile, to Katherine's dismay, they were obliged to have a civil wedding in the office of a magistrate, for newly planted Charles Towne as yet had no church in which to formalize their union, nor a priest to conduct it.

"My love," Phillip assured her, "there are plans afoot to build an Anglican church here, and I hear it will be called St. Phillip, my namesake. When it is ready we shall solemnize anew our vows there, if that is to your liking."

"Oh, Phillip, yes, it is indeed very much to my liking!"

Due to repairs and a lack of skilled carpenters needed to convert the *Kingston Elizabeth* into a cargo vessel, Phillip's voyage to Barbados was delayed until October, time enough for Katherine to discover that she was carrying her third child. She was thrilled, but Phillip seemed troubled by her happy revelation. His unexpected attitude stung her.

"I hoped you should be happy with the news I bring you, my darling. We have spoken often of a child. Are you then displeased?"

"No, no, my love, of course not. The news you bring me is cause for great joy, but it renders all the clearer my meager means and my dependence on your estate and admirable generosity;

and not least it is an unpleasant reminder that it came from Richard Blackwell, a man who wished my death. I am uncomfortable with my profitless state. I had hoped that by now my proposed commerce with Barbados would be thriving, but, alas, repair and restructuring of the vessel have been maddeningly slow."

"Do not concern yourself, dear husband. Materially we are well off and think not of how my estate came to be. Richard is gone from our lives, and now that we are married, my property belongs to you. Henry and Mary are happy and soon coming to fulfillment is my greatest desire, which has always been to give birth to your child, our child. And now that God has blessed us, you can without concern delay the voyage until my time is up and I deliver God's gift to our union."

"No, my love, on the contrary, the added, "family responsibility makes it all the more pressing for me to place on firm footing my proposed commercial venture in Barbados, particularly since the storm season is nearly over and my uncles may depart any day for England. I have gathered a good crew and shall sail to Barbados and return before the child is born. And we shall make sure you have maids and help aplenty to attend you in every need and desire while I am at sea."

"My governing desire is to have you by my side always," she said with a pucker of disappointment.

"And so you shall, and so you shall, my love. I shall return soon."

But he did not return, late or soon. After the storm season was past, He sailed away of a morning in late October with a cargo of cypress and pine lumber and Katherine never saw him again.

She was disturbed when she discovered that Phillip had taken much of her jewelry and most of her funds. But she told herself that he took them as a precaution against what might chance unexpectedly on the voyage. Had she not assured him that all was his? Yet as the weeks lengthened into months she could no longer keep at bay a terrible suspicion of deception.

November passed, and December came with its cold miasmic airs. Both children were ailing, suffering in their tender flesh, as she imagined, the affliction that was swelling in her heart. On warmer days she would walk to the harbor with her new black maids, Hannah and Ruth, to watch the vessels dock and put out to sea. Phillip may be marooned on an island, she told herself in moments of hope. Perhaps he lies wounded or captive, crying out for me as I send silent messages of love to him.

She sought information from seamen, but they had no knowledge of Phillip. Until finally a young Scottish sailor named Olgivie, newly arrived from Barbados after his indentured service, told her that the *Kingston Elizabeth* said to belong to a man by the name of Captain Stafford, as he recollected, had only a fortnight earlier sailed from the Bridgetown harbor.

"And this Captain Stafford, know you aught of him? She asked, trembling in uncontrollable nervousness.

"Why, ma'am, 'tis commonly bandied in Bridgetown that he lives as a principal gentleman on one of the French islands that neighbor Barbados—I disremember the name—residing thereon with a handsome estate, a great troop of servants, and a bonny wife. And though I saw his residence only through the glass as our vessel stood off becalmed in the sea lane, it was a pleasing sight indeed to the eye."

Katherine sagged in dizziness and her eyes clouded over.

Stout Hannah had to steady her as Ruth fanned her with her hand. She had no memory of returning to her residence or of retiring for the night.

The next morning dawned clear and cold, for winter lingered long and strong that year. Not that she noticed in her befuddled state. Rare frost covered the neighboring rooftops. She went out on her veranda to look once more toward the docks, not to hope again for Phillip's return but to say goodbye and good riddance to his memory, and in bidding him farewell to think how she was to live the rest of her life. Unthinking, she had stepped out barefoot on the cold deck and finally became aware that she was shivering, and her feet were cold. Then Sir Henry's oracular words came back once more to her in full force: "In a trice would hee traipse away to other adventures, leaving thee shivering in cold neglect."

After much sobbing and tears generously shed, Katherine declared an end to her grief and stoically accepted her situation. She declared herself a widow, explaining that her husband had vanished at sea somewhere in the Lesser Antilles. She was concerned about her dwindling funds but by force of will determined to put the problem out of her mind until she should be delivered of child. Jeremy was born in February, nearly six months after Phillip's disappearance. He much resembled his father. Despite her determination to put Phillip out of her thoughts and heart, sometimes tears would come to her eyes as she lovingly caressed and kissed the handsome babe.

Hannah and Ruth were devoted and competent. Sharing Sir Henry's philosophy that no man had the right to enslave another, Katherine granted them their freedom but retained their services by paying them a small wage she could barely afford but which soothed her conscience.

To her good fortune she gained the steadfast friendship of several English ladies, especially Mrs. Elizabeth Clifford and Mrs. Sarah Bankhead, who attended her during her gravid state and helped to see to her needs at Jeremy's birth. Carpenters and masons were building St. Phillip Church and a growing Anglican congregation impatiently awaited its completion and the arrival of an English rector. In the meantime, as best they could, they held informal prayer services in private homes, including Katherine's spacious residence.

Spurred by concern over her financial straits, it occurred to Katherine to act on an off-hand comment by Sarah Bankhead that Katherine's fluency in French was convenient for the community and perhaps could be profitable. Accordingly, she took steps to establish an academy that would offer classes in French for the children of English families and classic literary works for more advanced students. Back on her feet and fully active after a week, but down to a mere residue of funds, she interviewed and hired two young French Huguenot sisters, Claire and Beatrice Pontneuf to serve as teachers. English authorities barred French Catholics from Charles Towne but tolerated the French-speaking Huguenot Protestants. At first she set aside two large rooms in her residence as classrooms, but thanks to Sarah and Elizabeth enrollments quickly increased beyond her expectations, and as the school earned a respectable reputation with the better families, she leased a larger building. Within a year her income more than sufficed for her family and she was a much respected and appreciated member of Charles Town society.

Even more beautiful as a woman than she had been as a girl, Katherine was obliged to fend off a queue of devoted suitors. Her broken heart mended, but she did her best to convince herself that there would never be a place in it for new sentiments. For the most part her life continued in this peaceful and prosperous way for years until an event beyond her wildest dreams again drastically altered her life.

Part III

Four years passed and Katherine's French Academy for young ladies grew apace with Charles Towne itself. Her financial status was now secure, and she was socially established and respected as owner and headmistress of her flourishing school. The turmoil she had endured in Hampton and in the first months of residence in Charles Towne, though it had left no outward effect on her remarkable physical beauty, inwardly moderated her inclination to fanciful, girlish dreams of love and romance. Despite her love of things French, she now felt herself to be more English than ever before, and hereditary practicality was the stabilizing feature of her life as her youthful sentimentality faded. The shock of Phillip's betrayal and desertion had scarred her too deeply for full recovery and was an enduring buffer to new attractions. She did not waver in her resolve to spurn all amorous overtures from her many admirers. She admitted to herself that many among them were upstanding men of truth and morality — though others were enamored also of her growing wealth — but she was still too disillusioned to risk courtship and entertain their hopes. Then there were married men with their sly but obvious insinuations of willingness to comfort her. But she was content without being happy; the respect she enjoyed compensated to a degree for the decline of her youthful hopes of love and romance. There was comfort, if not happiness, in resignation to the placid emotional life to which fate had consigned her. Furthermore, the maternal fulfillment she enjoyed with her three splendid children enriched her life in an entirely different dimension. The compromise was not happiness, and certainly not balanced, for she was still a deeply passionate woman, but it resembled happiness enough to be a passable substitute. She could go on with her life. Motherhood, the academy, and public standing, not romantic love, were now her destiny.

Or so she reasoned to herself until February 10, 1684 when petite and pretty Claire fairly rushed into her office to announce that a gentleman wished urgently to speak with her.

"And the gentleman's name, Claire?" Katherine asked her in French. "Is he the father of one of our girls?"

"No, Madam, and I neglected to ask him his name, but he is very handsome!"

"And what is the nature of the handsome stranger's business with me?" Katherine asked her sarcastically.

"*Je ne le sais pas*, I know not, madam, only that he says it is urgent."

"Very well, Claire, show the gentleman in."

With that Katherine turned her back to the door and busied herself with other matters. She did not wish to seem eager to attend a total stranger, especially one who called unannounced. It had been a particularly trying day and she was not of a mind to waste her time with strangers. When Claire escorted him into the office, she waited a moment before turning to face him. Then upon seeing Phillip Stafford standing before her, she felt dizzy with rage and the room swam before her eyes. When she came fully to herself again, Claire and Beatrice were fanning her and rubbing her hands and face. Phillip kept his distance, but concern registered in his features. Katherine waved the young women away.

"Thank you, ladies, but I'm all right, just a moment of lightheadedness. Will you bring me a glass of water, please? And give me a moment alone with this man."

As both girls ran to fetch it, Katherine turned with cold fury in her eyes to confront Phillip.

"How dare you show your face here, miserable cad and scoundrel that you are!" she hissed, rising from her chair, eyes and features ablaze with anger. "Remove yourself at once and never darken my door again!"

"Madam, Madam, please calm yourself, I beg you," he responded in his soothing and familiar baritone voice. "I am not Phillip. I note with sadness, though not surprise, that my brother has done you some great wrong, as he has to so many persons, including our family. I must confess to you the obvious: Phillip is, or perhaps was by now, my twin brother. For I know nothing of what has become of him. I am, madam, David Stafford, at your service and the Savior's, and it is urgent that you permit me to explain the purpose of my visit, which is obviously as disturbing to you as the reason is painful for me."

Katherine interrupted her imprecations in mid-sentence as a look of doubt and puzzlement came over her features. "You, you are not Phillip?" she said hesitantly. Then angry at her own momentary credulity, she resumed her indignation in even harsher tones but in French: "*Montrez-moi la main droite, monsieur, et nous verrons si ce que vous dites est vrai ou faux*" (Show me your right hand, sir, and we shall see if what you say is true or false).

"My French is poor, madam, but I believe you told me to show you my right hand."

He dutifully held out his hand. The livid saber scar she remembered above his thumb was not there. Her eyes widened in surprise and astonishment. "Then it is true, you are not Phillip! But this is impossible!" she said, befuddled by the conflicting certainties her reason and her eyes were telling her.

"Nor am I his keeper, madam, only the redresser of some of his wrongs. We are both victims of his chicaneries, as are others in uncounted numbers. But these are sensitive matters better treated in private. Might we arrange a time and place to discuss them without undue disturbance or inadvertent ears to hear what must needs be said between us but spread no further?"

Though still agitated and not yet emotionally convinced that the man was not Phillip, Katherine could not disagree with his reasoning. Yet she was mindful of the commotion and gossip his presence could cause if he remained unidentified, or worse, if the pose turned out to be yet another deception and he was, after all, the husband whose death she had announced years earlier. Who he was and a justifiable reason for his presence in Charles Towne were matters that urgently needed to be clarified. Before any private conversation, however, it had to be made clear to as many of her friends and acquaintances as possible that this was her brother-in-law come to pay his respects to his widowed sister-in-law and her children, most particularly his nephew Jeremy. The best way to proceed, she decided, would be to gather intimate friends for a tea that very evening. It would be risky to delay. David did not object but rather understood and appreciated her foresight and concern for their respective reputations.

Although he did not display the seductive charm and savoir-faire of his brother, David impressed Katherine's friends with his compelling honesty and gentlemanly conduct. Those who remembered Phillip—and the curious included Katherine most of all—could not help staring at him, for his features and stature were duplicates of his brother's, and his resonant baritone voice stirred disturbing recollections of Phillip. Katherine was pleased and relieved when her friends left her house completely persuaded, as was she, that David Stafford had shown himself to be a trustworthy gentleman, and in the unconscious manner of the wealthy, a man of substance. Several of the men expressed their hope that this visit would not be his last to Charles Towne and that he might see fit to establish commercial links with the Carolina Colony. Such men, they said forcefully, were needful for the Colony to flourish.

Even though it was an effort for her to trust the man, at least her fears of gossip and misunderstanding were alleviated by the favorable impression her closest friends formed of David. She had no qualms in inviting him for dinner, for not to do so now that she was surely to be under scrutiny would stir gossip, just as too much familiarity could injure the good reputation she had worked so carefully to build. She introduced him to her children, who warmed spontaneously to his affectionate way with them. Mary and Jeremy happily sat in his lap.

Leaning on his knee, Henry looked up at him and to Katherine's embarrassment, asked hopefully, "Sir, are you our father? I think I remember your face from when I was a little boy."

"No, lad," he replied, smiling and draping an arm across Henry's shoulders, "I am your Uncle David. But I hope we shall have other occasions to deepen our family ties and become good friends, for I see that you are a strong and handsome lad indeed."

By the time the children were asleep, Katherine was

beginning to trust David. They talked well into the evening hours. Carefully choosing her words and artfully omitting complicity in any tawdry details, she explained some of circumstances surrounding her relationship with Phillip.

"I cannot express the sorrow I feel for the pain and unhappiness Phillip brought you, dear Katherine," he responded. "But neither am I surprised to learn of it. If I may speak boldly to the matter, Phillip's conduct deviates not in the least from the pattern of deception common to all his affairs I know of. In my particular case, I act principally on behalf of my two maternal uncles and two younger siblings but am mindful of other misdeeds, some directed against me, and no doubt ignorant of many others for which he must answer, in this life or the next. It is with great sadness that I must speak thusly of my brother, my twin. In physical appearance we exhibit only similarities, but God forbid that I should ever be tempted to tread the dark pathways he chooses. I am by no means a perfect man, but I try to act honorably in all my affairs."

"Phillip spoke of his uncles in Barbados and of their intention to take retirement in England."

"That intention, Katherine, innocently confessed to my brother, led him to commit one of his most despicable misdeeds."

"How so?" she asked, dreading to hear more of Phillip's misdeeds but moved by a morbid curiosity about a man she had loved deeply and now vehemently despised.

"It seems that Phillip began his deception by presenting himself as me, as David Stafford, to my Uncles. They knew something of Phillip's wayward life and being men of honor would not have allowed him into their confidence. But they had, I dare say, a favorable memory and impression of me. And this led to the calamity that I shall describe directly. My Uncles knew I had resettled myself in Boston and we maintained sporadic correspondence via distant kinfolk in England. But ignorant of Phillip's whereabouts, at first none of us had knowledge of you or the children. God only knows what fabulous tales he told my trusting Uncles Alexander and William to carry out his swindle."

"Although I am loath to learn of it, what swindle was that, David?"

"By an unhappy coincidence of timing, I had written my Uncles that I desired to see more of the world, the whole of my existence having been spent in Stafford and Boston. Keenest among my hopes was the prospect of seeing them again after so many years. Having amassed a comfortable estate and without binding family ties in Boston or England, I mentioned that a voyage to Barbados was foremost on my listing of desirable destinations, though I hoped also to visit other islands and perhaps the southern mainland as well. In time I received correspondence from them in which they expressed their eagerness to see me. In some manner that is still unclear to me, they learned about you. I surmise that soon after he met you in Hampton and before his later schemes were still immature, Phillip so informed them with some particulars about your family. It was there I learned of your remove to Charles Towne where, at last, I have happily found you and your children."

"And what has become of your uncles and their intention to return to England?"

"Insofar as I can determine, it appears that Phillip pilfered their fortune by offering himself as their agent, using the unhappy coincidence of his visit, his exact physical resemblance to me, and their desire to return to their old homeland. He then disappeared, perhaps removing to Martinique or one of the islands in that region, leaving them near impoverishment in Barbados. The precise details of his mischief are unclear to me, but needless to say, their funds, placed trustingly in his hands, never reached England. Now I must with all possible haste proceed to the island to alleviate their plight as best I can."

"And what remedy do you foresee, if I may be so bold as to ask?"

"If they are of a mind to return to England and have strength for the voyage, I shall see that they are comfortably reestablished in old Stafford. On no account shall I abandon them in backward Barbados. Perhaps they will choose to live with me and my siblings Garth and Martha in Boston where I have a spacious, near-empty house, though I fear the New England winters might prove overly rigorous for them."

"From your remarks, I gather you have no family of your own, David. Are you not married?"

"No, I am not. When circumstances offered me a better chance at life in Boston I was engaged for marriage, but the lady who was to be my wife could not, at the final hour, bring herself to leave her parents and brave the ocean voyage and the uncertainties of life in America. She pleaded her youth and asked me for a greater grant of time. We parted in tearful sorrow and with hearty pledges of reunion and marriage in some happier day. But time eroded our young love and our pledges faded to melancholy memories. After some years we ceased to correspond, and I suppose that neither of us wished to continue to entertain sentiments that belonged to our youth but not to our future."

"What became of her?"

"I confess my ignorance of her fate, as she surely became

indifferent to mine. Forgive me for speaking of the matter at too great length."

"You must have cared deeply for her at one time."

"Indeed, so I did, or at least so fancied, which made our parting all the sadder for me. But after years of more mature reflection, I came to see that sentiments blinded us to an obvious truth: we both had many traits that did not promise a harmonious union. She was a gay girl, heartily fond of parties, dance and song, whereas I was concerned foremost with the work and responsibility of establishing myself."

"Stop me, David, if I ask questions that discomfit you, but were you ever again so deeply attracted to anyone?"

"No, not yet, but though I have not found love, I retain the hope that one day it will find me. But turnabout is fair play, Katherine, and surely your story is much more interesting than my plain life. From what I know and to judge by your handsome older children, I gather you were widowed before Phillip came into your life, were you not?"

"Yes, I was married to a man named Richard Blackwell not long after my Father and I left France for Hampton in the Virginia Colony. You will no doubt think me flighty, David, as indeed I was as a girl. In my young years my imagination was puffed up with vaporous sentimentalities, which prepared me only to be charmed witless by Phillip. I married Richard under protest only because my father pressured me into the union. But let me hasten to add, my father acted with the best of paternal intentions. Our family had lost almost everything meaningful in the Cromwell War, above all my two precious brothers, John and Pickford, may God rest their souls. After my mother's death in France when fortune and favor had long since abandoned him and he knew that he, too, must soon leave this world, my father had as his remaining desire to see me conveniently wed. I had not the heart to oppose him even if it meant sacrificing what I errantly believed to be my own happiness."

"I surmise, then, that the union with Mr. Blackwell was not altogether a happy one."

"No, not at first, though later it was bearable and at least I had my darling children Henry and Mary after his tragic death. And of my marriage to Phillip was born sweet little Jeremy. They and the Academy fill my life."

Not many days thereafter before Katherine and the children, David said farewell. All were teary-eyed, for during his short stay, mutual affections had grown strong. David took passage on an outbound ship for Barbados. Beyond that destination, plans were unmade and dependent on the wishes and health of his uncles. In any case, as soon as possible, whether measured in weeks or months, he must return to his affairs in Boston. Charles Towne had impressed him most favorably, particularly his conversations with town leaders regarding commercial needs and possibilities in the young colony. Nevertheless, when, if ever, he might make another trip to Carolina, though high among the hopes of all assembled, was unforeseeable and for the moment, unlikely.

Katherine soon resumed the former balance of life with the children, the Academy, and her circle of friends, but she could not so readily recapture the tranquility she had known before David's visit. The initial shock and anger that his physical resemblance to Phillip aroused in her soon gave way to cordiality and appreciation, though not without leaving a residue of agitation in her spirit. She cherished her female friends and coolly kept several respectable admirers at arm's length, but David reminded her how much her life could be enriched by trustworthy men—if such there were—who would offer genuine friendship and respect for her emotional boundaries. She had endured a loveless union with Richard and adored Phillip with a consuming passion in the other. Yet she remembered both marriages with hurt and humiliation and determined never again to open her heart to love. The world saw her as a wealthy and beautiful woman, and not even those closest to her could sense all the bitterness and hurt she harbored for the way life that had mocked her youthful idealism. The girl she once was still yearned to be cherished, but the mature woman she had become distrusted every romantic impulse. Not that she cast all the blame on others; her own impulsive sentimentality was foremost in fault.

The languorous summer of 1685 passed, and autumn was nearly spent before a schooner brought to Charles Towne a post from David. Presently in England, he was arranging a comfortable living for his Uncle William Woolsey in Stafford. Sadly, his elder Uncle Alexander did not live to see his homeland again but died only a fortnight after David arrived in Barbados. From nothing David wrote, but by hints in his correspondence, Katherine deduced that as he feared, he found them reduced to near penury and too old and exhausted to rebuild their fortunes. David entreated his uncle William to remove to Boston so as to be with his closest kin, but though the old gentleman was grateful, Mother England made the stronger appeal.

"My remaining days in this world go dwindling in number, dear David, and I should like to complete the cycle of my life, ending it where it began, in dear old Stafford. Besides, from what

I hear of the harsh winters of New England, I fear the cold would hasten my demise. At this point in my life I have no other compelling wish and but one regret: that Alexander was unable to share these last days with me."

David repeated how delightful it had been to meet her, Henry, Mary, and Jeremy, and to make the acquaintance of so many good people of Charles Towne. He closed with these words: "For me it was a delightful visit of which I preserve cherished memories and one I should like to repeat if God grants me time enough and chance. Were it merely up to me, I should as quickly as possible bend my steps southward again. So man dreams and proposes, but at the last God decides and disposes. In any case, I must complete living arrangements with my remaining kin for my Uncle William here in Stafford, then sail for Boston to put my affairs in good order before untried matters foremost in my mind may be contemplated."

She wondered what he meant by these vague words: '. . . before any untried matters in my mind may be contemplated'. What "untried matters" did he mean? But time passed, and her curiosity diminished under the press of daily, mundane chores. In any case, she told herself, it was an idle matter without consequence. Although she would have welcomed him, she told herself several times that probably she had seen David for the first and last time.

But on a Tuesday afternoon in late May, petite Beatrice fairly ran in to Katherine's office breathless with the news: "Madame, Monsieur Stafford *est revenu*, he has returned! He is here!" Katherine barely had time to smooth her hair and compose herself before David stood smiling in the doorway. Later she would scold Beatrice for her undignified comportment in his hearing, but she could barely control her own excitement and pleasure upon seeing him again.

"Forgive me, dear Katherine, for arriving without giving you prior notice, perhaps warning would be a choicer word. No doubt you have perceived that calling unannounced is one of my many shortcomings. In my eagerness to see you and receive word of the children again, I hied myself directly here from the wharf. I should have taken lodging first and then sent word to you. I hope my presence is not a burdensome intrusion. And by the by," he added with a chuckle, extending his right hand, "as you can see, it has no scar. I am myself, that is, still myself."

"So I noticed, David," Katherine answered with a smile, "but I needed no such proof this time to know that you are the same dear gentleman the children and I met last year. And far from an intrusion, much less a burden, your visit is a most welcome surprise," she said, taking him by the hands and planting phantom kisses on each cheek in the French manner.

"I shall not long detain you from your tasks, Katherine. My porters await me outside with my trunks, and even now men are unlading my possessions from the ship. But to the main point: are all well? Are the children in good health, as you, by your appearance, evidently are?"

"Indeed, David, we are all well, thanks be to God. But what of you? We shall be eager to learn all the many things that have befallen you in your several destinations since you took your leave from us last year."

"And I with the same curiosity wish to learn what has happened here in Charles Towne, which I see has grown apace. But first, I must hasten back to attend to matters of lodging and storage. The porters will grow impatient if I tarry longer."

"You speak as though your visit will be long, as we hope."

"On that particular and others there is much to say. But I beg you, let us delay that conversation until we are at our leisure to discuss them."

The opportunity came that very afternoon. David was comfortably lodged in Travelers Inn and his possessions stored in Gilmore's warehouse near the wharf. Katherine invited him for tea and a reunion with her close friends, many of whom he recalled from his earlier visit.

"We are delighted to see you again in Charles Towne, Mr. Stafford," said haberdasher Bernard Clifford. "You will no doubt recall our collective hope that you might see fit to establish commercial links with Charles Towne. Remark how it has grown since your visit a year ago. May we now expect, sir, to hear the welcome news that you have favorably entertained our hope?"

"You may indeed, sir, if all do welcome the news," he responded with a quick glance at Katherine. "Not only do I intend to establish those connections but also to take up residence in this fair city."

"That is indeed good news to us all, Mr. Stafford," Mr. Clifford smilingly assured him. "Our community needs enterprising men of means to assure its future. I dare say I speak for all here that we welcome you and offer our assistance if we may be of service to you in any way."

"Hear! Hear!" said a chorus of voices.

"Katherine, we have not heard from you," said Mrs. Bankhead. "What do you think of your brother-in-law's intention to remove to Charles Towne?"

"I was thinking most directly of the children and recalling how quickly they grew fond of David last year, I celebrate his return." Then turning to David, she added: "The children have asked me many times about you, David. And now that they have heard of your arrival, I doubt not that this evening you shall have a welcoming committee of eager small folk to greet you. It will be most convenient for them to have a man's influence in the family."

"I shall strive to be a good influence on them without being an inconvenience for you, Katherine."

Several of the women, though perhaps none of the men, noticed a slight tremor in his voice and a faint respondent color that came to her cheeks.

Rector Jonathan Meeks spoke to his particular interest and turned the conversation in another direction. "I shall welcome you into our worship at St. Phillips, Mr. Stafford. You are, I shall assume, a member in good standing in our Mother Church."

"Father Meeks, through no merit of mine but by the grace of God I am in harmony with the Church, and may God grant that I continue to be faithful in worship and service here as I was in Boston and have been since my boyhood in England."

It was evident from the frown that creased his face that Father Meeks was not pleased with something in the tone or turn of David's words. But he murmured perfunctorily, "I perceive, therefore, Mr. Stafford, that you acknowledge no obstacle that would hinder you from becoming a devoted servant of our Lord at St. Phillip. I shall hope that such is the case."

The comment, proper in words but cold in tone, chilled the easy cordiality that had prevailed at tea and replaced it with a tension with obvious effects but without reasonable cause. Not long thereafter the guests began leaving. David was taken aback by the Rector's oblique, frosty tone and wondered what he had said that could have offended the clergyman. Later, when they alone he asked Katherine about it.

"Do not fret over the matter, David. Perhaps it will soothe your feelings somewhat to learn that Father Meeks has said similar things to many of us, myself included. There is a distressing coldness in his character that dismays many of us. In my case, the untidy circumstance of a having as a parishioner a woman twice a wife and twice a relict seems to annoy him greatly. We—and I believe I speak for all—have come to consider his peculiarities a sort of diffidence and a personal shortcoming of Father Meeks and for the good of the Church try to overlook it."

Before their bedtime, Henry, Mary, and Jeremy showed how delighted they were to have an uncle in their midst and asked him several times as they climbed on his knees if he really intended to live in Charles Towne.

"Yes, I do intend to live here, and I know of no circumstance that makes me happier than to have about me two stout nephews and a pretty niece to bring enjoyment to my life. We shall have good times together. But you shall have to teach me your games. I am an old bachelor unused to fun but willing to learn. Will you then teach me how to play your games?"

"Yes!" they said as one.

"I shall show you how to play ball," exclaimed Henry. "It's not hard to learn."

"If you don't know how to play tag, Uncle David, Jeremy and I shall show you. Shan't we, Jeremy?" added Mary.

"Yes, but you're not too old to run, are you, Uncle David? Asked little Jeremy.

"Oh, I think I can still run a bit," David laughed, "but maybe not so fast as you, Jeremy. For I see that you are a good stout lad."

"David, you have won over the children in a masterful way," Katherine told him later when they were alone. "One would think you have had a long experience with children."

"Unhappily no, as you are aware, but with your blessing I intend to be a good uncle to these three."

"To all three?" she asked timidly. "I understand in the case of Jeremy, but Henry and Mary . . .?"

"I claim them all without distinction of blood relationship but with equal affection, if it please you, Katherine."

"Oh, David, it does please me very much, more than I can tell you. How generous of you."

"No, Katherine, you are the generous one to allow me to be an uncle to these beautiful little ones. But before I get carried away with that pleasant prospect, we shall have to see whether I really can run at tag and play ball," he laughed.

As the summer passed their conversations became more relaxed and intimate, though ever circumspect and respectful. David explained to Katherine that his circumstances in Boston had become increasingly stressful since his return from England. Garth, his younger brother, with whom he had partnered in various enterprises since their arrival in Boston, now chaffed under his directorship and felt a growing urge to control his own entrepreneurial fortunes, particularly in shipbuilding and shipping. In this their sister Martha sided with Garth, who was close to her in age and character. Finally, it became painfully clear to all that a change was inevitable. David then proposed a buyout much to the advantage of his younger siblings. They agreed, and the transaction was completed without serious disruption of family harmony.

Meanwhile, as a transitional measure, David purchased two commercial buildings in Charles Towne for the purpose of leasing warehouse space to solid enterprises in order to provide himself a convenient and substantial income. But his eventual plans were more elaborate. He explained to Katherine and mentioned to some in her circle of friends that as soon as he was sufficiently at ease in Charles Towne and knowledgeable with the region, he intended not only to become a land broker but to set aside planation tracts for cultivation under his personal supervision.

"What sort of cultivation have you in mind?" Katherine inquired when they were alone.

"Rice, for one. With its mild climate, abundant water, and improving shipping facilities, this country is proving to be ideal for growing that grain."

"But, David, and I ask this with respect, have you the required experience? You have spent your life in Boston and England, and I cannot image growing rice in either place."

"Neither can I," he laughed, "but I am in a position and lately of a disposition to try new things. Rice farming is one of them, and I may also try indigo. It will require adjustments for me to become a planter, but I believe it will prove lucrative."

"Have you still other new ventures in mind?"

"Yes, several, but one above all others and indeed much more personal."

"If it is not an indiscretion to ask, what might it be?"

"Matrimony."

"Matrimony? Did I hear you correctly? I thought bachelorhood was a confirmed way of life for you."

"I long thought so myself. Yet you recall that in early

manhood I proposed marriage to a young woman in England. Her rejection of my suit sent my life along a different course, which altered but did not displace my early conviction that marriage was a better state than the single life."

"Since you have affirmed your intention so directly, may I assume that you have a lady in mind?"

"Indeed, you may assume so, Katherine. In my heart I have chosen the lady, but it remains to be seen whether she will have me."

"Do I know her?"

"Intimately."

"Are you willing to reveal her name?"

"I see no reason to keep it from you. Her name is Katherine."

"Katherine, but that is my name and I know of no other 'Katherine' in our circle of friends. She is then, I take it, a resident of Boston."

"No, I know no one by that name in Boston. But let me demur no longer. You, dearest Katherine, are the lady, and I shall be the happiest and most honored man on God's good earth if you will accept me as your husband."

She stared at him for a moment, then lowered her eyes as they moistened with tears. He touched her arm affectionately, but she turned her face and pulled away.

"Dear Katherine, I did not mean to cause you anguish, and I regret that without so intending, it seems that I have. My love for you took root a year ago and has grown without surcease since then. It is genuine and strong, and if there be any honor or truth in me, these are the qualities that move me to make this declaration of my love and petition of marriage to you. Yet poorly versed in matters of the heart and a mere bumbler in my treatment of women, I see that I have offended you. I ask your forgiveness."

"Oh, David," she said, daubing her eyes with a handkerchief, "you have not offended me. Stunned and surprised me, yes, but offended me, no. But marriage is out of the question. Our circumstances would not allow it even if I were worthy to be your wife. Consider the principal obstacle: we are family. Your brother was, and mayhap still is so legally, my husband. You know some of the unhappy circumstances of my life. I had my chances for happiness and either my poor choices or fate put an unhappy end to them."

"I respect your thinking but for good reasons soundly reject your objections. Everything you have said I have repeated to myself a thousand times. As for the 'principal obstacle', as you call it, I have dwelt on it longest. Leaving aside your first marriage, which has no direct bearing on the matter, there are two reasons that invalidate it. First, Phillip either married you under false pretenses or, second, abandoned you years ago. Either circumstance is enough to free you of any and all legal ties to him, living or deceased. Consider his relationship to you a foreshadowing, a false simulacrum, of a true marriage that I now propose to you. If I may speak even more boldly, the shadow he cast was empty and dark like all shadows, but our life together can be the substance his falsified life lacked. I have discussed all these matters with legal authorities and they corroborate everything I tell you. English law is clear on the point of abandonment provided the requisite number of years have passed, as indeed they have."

"But the Church would still view us as in-laws, which is as prohibitive a relationship as brother and sister, so I understand."

"No, dear Katherine, for the same reasons that our code of Common Law can set aside a marriage as I described, so the Church can similarly void an invalid union or annul it in cases of abandonment. In any case, a civil ceremony, while valid in the eyes of the Church in common practice, may in this instance with greater expediency be set aside, if need be. Strictly speaking, Katherine, at this late date you and I are not in-laws, which means that we may, as consenting adults, enter into the state of matrimony, which will be binding and permanent in the eyes of the Church so long as we both shall live. And it is this union that I propose and ask you to accept."

"I tremble to think what Father Meeks would say if we were to approach him on the subject. No doubt he would refuse to allow such a ceremony in a most fulminating and demeaning manner."

"Luckily, my dear, Father Meeks is Rector only of St. Phillip's, not the Church of England. There are other, wiser priests than that shallow fellow."

"David, would you really wish to marry a woman like me?" she asked.

"No, my darling, not a woman like you, but you yourself. And not only do I wish with all my heart to be your husband but desire further to be a father to your children."

"To all of them? Not just Jeremy . . .?"

"I believe we settled that question some time ago. What I said as their uncle, I repeat as their prospective father. I do not believe I speak in vain when I say that the children have rendered a verdict in my favor, albeit," David added with a chuckle, "stout Henry and spritely Jeremy make light of my clumsiness of foot in our games of ball and tag. And pretty Mary laments my dullness of wit because my memory falters at recalling the names of all her dolls."

Her eyes still glistened with tears, but a smile brightened her face. "You joke of course; Henry adores you, as do Mary and Jeremy. But on the main point, David, I have determined never again to entertain thoughts of marriage. And there we must leave the matter. You have won my confidence and respect, and, yes, my affection and gratitude also as a friend, but my heart must remain closed to other feelings. Now, with all these feelings firm and foremost, I consider the matter settled and must ask you to leave me."

David rose at once, bowed, and with unusually curt words, "as you wish, Katherine," left after a few whispered words to Hanna as she opened the door for him. Katherine wondered if she had spoken too harshly and offended him. Another conflictive agitation, she sighed, to the many he had aroused in her.

But in the coming days and weeks, she discovered that if David was more circumspect in his methods because of her rebuff, he was undismayed in his eventual purpose. He pressed his suit with attentions paid her at every opportunity. She rejoiced in his affection for her children, for true to his word, he loved them generously and equally. Gradually her guard relaxed. In the abstract she still looked with horror on the thought of matrimony, but David loomed ever larger in her feelings. She was as adamant as ever against another marriage, but she had come to need and depend on David's steady support and friendship. As for her other suitors, she was less interested than ever in listening to their pleas and pledges. To make matters worse, Bernard Clifford, husband of her closest friend Elizabeth, was becoming so obvious in his sly insinuations that Katherine knew she must soon put a stop to them. But how? Elizabeth was devoted to her husband and would not believe the derogatory truth about him. To speak out would mean ridding herself of his advances but most likely at the sacrifice of her friendship with Elizabeth and the ugly possibility that the matter would find its way into public gossip. She did nothing at the time but fretted all the more in private.

One day the chilling thought occurred to her: what if David wearies of my rejection and leaves? Or turns to another woman for the affection I cannot give him? She spent a sleepless night with these bedeviling thoughts. To make matters worse, the very next day David told her that he must return to Boston and thence perhaps to England. His answers to her inquiries were so general as to be evasive, and Katherine was left with another cause for mounting agitation. She reassured herself that his departure was for commercial reasons, as he hinted, and that he should, God willing, make a timely return to Charles Towne. But then dark fears assailed her logic and she had to fight against the idea that he might never return. He had proposed honorable matrimony to her, and she, ever the fool, had rejected him. Would she never learn anything in matters of love? Already a matron in years, she berated herself for being sentimentally still a foolish girl half her age.

Four months later, an eternity for her, David returned, informing her that pending matters in Boston were finally resolved. The last commercial leases held in common with Garth had expired. With a joy she could barely conceal, Katherine heard his pledge that from now on he would settle himself in Charles Towne and, undistracted, was more determined than ever to pursue his interests in Carolina.

Worn out by emotional turmoil, neither womanly modesty nor sentimental fear could keep her from asking him the tormenting questions: "David, have your interests changed? Do they still include rice and matrimony?"

For the briefest instant he was surprised by her bluntness. Then sensing victory in her obvious anxiety, he smiled, took her by the hand and kissed it.

"More than ever, dear Katherine, more than ever. But before I plant rice in the fields, I hope to see it showered on my head in a wedding ceremony."

"Forgive my forwardness, David, but does your lady of choice remain the same?"

"For me there can be none other on earth. You, beloved Katherine, are, and always shall be, the possessor of my heart. How answer you now to my proposal of marriage?"

"The only answer I can give, dear David. In the days and months since we last spoke of the matter, my heart with its reasons has overruled my head with its logic, as my beloved Pascal forewarned. My world is upside down. But there is a higher logic to it after all. For plain reason and common sense cannot gainsay the fact that in the hierarchy of affections 'husband' has a far sweeter ring to it than 'brother-in-law'. Against my rational judgment and in despite of the alarums and caveats of my head and old sentimental wounds, Master Stafford, yes, I will marry you. It may seem immodest of me, but I shall confess to you that sentiments which began as cordial admiration of your qualities and affection for your person have deepened in these weeks and months into a love I cannot deny, nor do I have any reason or wish to do so. When I first confronted these feelings, I could not imagine life with you; now, dear David, I confess that I cannot bear the thought of life without you."

"Then save for pending particulars, dearest Katherine, the matter is settled. Surely you knew with the canny insight of your sex that I fell in love with you the first time I met you. You, dear Katherine, are now the resplendent light of my once solitary life, the joy of today and the happy expectation of tomorrow. Now I have a reason to live and to rejoice in life. I shall love you forever."

"And a day?" she smiled as she came to him to accept his embrace.

"Forever and a day," he echoed as he kissed her for the first time.

War Bride

Madelaine-Marie DuCordier-Stokes described her first impressions of the American soldiers at several family gatherings after her marriage to Captain Dan Stokes. She was not quite twenty-one when the first American tanks rolled into Rouen followed by lines of soldiers behind each one. At first the French populace, weary of German oppression and wary of all soldiers, was not sure how they should react to the new invaders, although word had reached them that the Yanks, though heavy drinkers, had a reputation for benign treatment of the civilian populations. Nevertheless, at first the French were sullenly resentful that aside from the good or ill intentions of the Americans, foreign forces still controlled the destinies of France.

It was not only a matter of pride and humiliation. The retreating Germans not only had taken with them almost all available goods and food but also in obedience to vindictive orders had destroyed the means of distributing any that were left. Rouen faced starvation. The Nazi crime was the final outrage in a list too long and shameful to report. Would the Americans now repeat those atrocities?

French apprehensions were soon laid to rest. The loud, boisterous Americans quickly began to distribute food, water, clothing, blankets, and basic commodities to the hungry citizens with smiles, shouts, and incredible largesse. The French, though heirs of a thousand-year-tradition of Gallic skepticism, were soon won over and came to look on the Yanks not as conquerors but as liberators in the noblest meaning of the word. With few exceptions, the Americans behaved more like oversized, playground boys than grim soldiers. Most knew only a few catchphrases of French and almost nothing of French history. They drank not to enjoy the wine but to get drunk and ate not to appreciate the cuisine but only to fill their stomachs. Refinement was not their calling. Compared to the Germans, even the common foot soldiers, they were as oblivious as children to the old European canons of art, music, food, and culture. But they compensated for their vast ignorance and exuberant barbaric behavior by their much greater human qualities of generosity and optimism. And the French could only marvel at their creative ingenuity.

Madelaine had nodded in agreement with the words of an admired French intellectual of that era who said of the Americans, "The Germans, like other despotic nations before them, set out to conquer Europe and the world. Were the Americans imbued with the Nietzschean will to power, they might really accomplish what other great tyrants tried but failed to do. Yet the idea is self-contradictory: for if they were to set their mind on world conquest, it would cost them their youthful freedom of spirit, which is the secret of their ingenuity and true power. Let them be as they are, and as long as they are so, we shall all be the better for it."

Young Madelaine was as *éblouie*, as dazzled, as her countrymen by these brash, irrepressible Americans who appealed to the youthfulness of each person, lately forgotten by young and old alike under the duress of war and oppression. Matronly and grandfatherly French faces etched by care, smiled again. Once more, light reached corners of the French soul sealed up for years. It is true that some French smiles concealed secret scorn primped to imitate a friendly face. Their ancestral skepticism held on tenaciously. The Americans did not notice, did not care, and would have taken it as a thing of no consequence if they had known the difference. They had no talent for nuances, and least of all for delicate jabs inspired by secret animosities.

Madelaine, who had read much, saw in the young Americans a kinship to the extinct heroes of old Europe. Once medieval knights and champions had strutted with the same unconcerned abandon. Like the Americans, they had sat, spat and pissed where they pleased and walked the world with the fierce, unpretentious happiness of being themselves. They knew and generally respected larger laws, but their first loyalty was to their own self-worth. Later ages would give it the coded, abstract names of honor and integrity, but at the primal, unrefined level of early times it was simply the unfeigned pride and privilege of being free men and the willingness to defend it under all circumstances.

Madelaine saw old Europe reincarnated in a new generation of large, loud and lusty barbarians from the West. In America, Europe's offspring, she believed herself to be a witness to the revival of the European spirit, not in refinement of the cultured taste and appreciation of modern times but in the primitive energy of its medieval warriors and champions that undergirded later refinement.

But as she was to discover later, there was a danger in giving free rein to her grandiose philosophic comparisons. These soldiers were comparable but not identical to her idolized old European knights, and young America was not Europe reincarnated, though an ancestral bond between them remained that neither continent could safely sever. Madelaine recolored her world with idyllic images, for tarnished after years of warfare, it was too sordid and horrific to command her full loyalty. She took to heart and expanded a conviction rooted in her readings that no world and no person is fully real without their poetic dimensions, and she luxuriated in the soothing conviction that every human life is a new metaphorical creation. It gave dignity to everything human teetering on the brink of annihilation yet required of her no vast commitment in return. Madelaine did not like sudden strenuous efforts of mind or body, nor things that came uncomfortably close to her private world of ideals and fantasies. Hundreds of years earlier her DuCordier ancestors had intermarried with English aristocracy, and she wondered if Anglo-Saxon genetic remnants had something to do with her need for withdrawal and ample personal space and silence. These moments alternately thrilled and frightened her, for they seemed to threaten her Gallic and Latin side that lived and longed for company and conversation. It was a conflict she chose not to explore or resolve, preferring the mystery of uncertainty to the rulings of clear-headed thinking. Like all Frenchmen, she understood and claimed as her own the diamantine reasoning of Descartes, but she was too much a child of the Nordic world to be an ever-faithful disciple of his logic. Stranded between two worlds—or so she imagined herself—she did not worship nature like a true Romantic, or even less as a rational Deist. Her favorite vistas were not lofty physical mountains or actual seas—though she had a respectable artistic appreciation of such sights—but insights and voyages on oceans that flowed from her spirit.

She had grown up amid luxuries, music, literature, art, and

sophisticated philosophies of a bygone world, and though these had been stripped from her life, she saw no reason to restrict herself to the commonplace, though she accommodated it. Insofar as she could, and as long as she could, she held her conflictive inclinations in a kind of tentative balance. She was too wise to hope for a definitive truce, much less a clear triumph of one dimension or the other, instead she reconciled herself to the inevitability that everything human falls apart, as it must, so that, as she believed in happier times, it can be recreated, or, as she feared in gloomier moments, it can revert to nothingness.

In a less definitive form, these were some of the general patterns of her existential thoughts when she met and, at the urging of her fearful father, married Captain Dan Stokes in August of 1945. She did not try to explain her thoughts to him for she knew that he would not understand them, any more than one of her medieval knights would have understood the subtleties that developed centuries after his life. Their only common ground was his desires and feelings flowing in high hormonal flood. Dan Stokes desired her as only a young, hot-blooded man can lust for the evasive beauty of an exotic woman who seemed ever just beyond his grasp. Madelaine was younger, yet he thought of her as older than he. She did not avoid him yet did not offer herself entirely then or later. He regretted angrily, yet manfully kept his hasty promise to respect her virginity until they could live together as husband and wife in California.

Language was an incidental problem in their relationship. All the DuCordiers spoke a degree of European English, especially Madelaine, who had studied piano and literature in England for two years. But at times the two versions of the language did not mesh, and Dan, who knew no French, was too limited in his own language and education to grasp some things they told him.

He left for America a week after their wedding. Claude DuCordier, Madelaine's father, was in frail health and lacked the stamina to confront and resolve convoluted matters of the family's several estates, including defiant squatters on some of them and foreign accounts in London and Switzerland. Her mother Madame Angelique, whose father taught her that women did not concern themselves with business matters, took his teaching as dogma. This left Madelaine herself, Louis, her underage brother, 17, and older brother Marc, 26, who when last heard from had settled in Algeria and vowed never to return to France. The agreement was struck: Captain Stokes would return to America and Madelaine would attend to pressing family matters and follow him within the year.

And so she did in October of 1946. After three days of train travel from New York she reached San Francisco. There, fatigued from lack of sleep and bewildered by the strangeness of everything she saw, she found her way to a bus station and completed the four-hour ride to Redding.

Danny was nowhere to be seen as she scrutinized the welcoming crowd. Her arrival was something of an epiphany for the thirty-odd townspeople on the platform. Dan was a decorated local hero, and the townspeople, who had heard exaggerated stories about Madelaine's links to French nobility, were ready to treat her as visiting royalty. Immediately they offered to show her the town and points of interest. Madelaine was astonished at their apparent indifference to her fatigue and need to rest. Since they were not tired, it did not occur to them that anyone else would be. Someone had remembered that one of the local men had married a German girl named Helga and trotted her out to meet Madelaine as though they had everything in common. The two women shook hands and mumbled pleasantries that neither felt, then turned aside to the disappointment of the sponsors who expected them to bond like two long-lost sisters. Weren't they both from Europe?

Jasper and Henrietta Stokes made their way through the crowd to greet and rescue their mysterious daughter-in-law. Jasper was shorter than Captain Dan but with some of the same facial features. Henrietta was nearly as tall as Dan and probably as heavy as her husband, blue-eyed and fair with once-blond hair now fading into gray.

"And Dan, Madame Stokes, is he here?" asked Madelaine.

"Oh, we didn't get your message until late yesterday. Danny's enrolled in the University of Oregon, up in Eugene."

"I didn't know," Madelaine said softly, wondering why Dan had not mentioned it in his brief letters.

"Well, he just started this fall," she said as though it were the most natural thing in the world. "He was expecting you in November, but he'll be home in two weeks. Or you could join him in Eugene. It's not too far. He has a nice little apartment close to the University. I think the two of you would be comfortable there. And Eugene is a nice university town with a lot of things to see and do."

Madelaine was unsure where she stood. Henrietta seemed nice enough, but Jasper was not as welcoming. A thought occurred to Madelaine: two people can love each other, but their cultures may not have any love for each other. She thought of Helga and wondered if they would ever be friends, or if Helga would be happy with an American husband. Maybe she and Helga did have something in common: the negatives of their circumstances. She was several years older than Madelaine but seemed lost and forlorn, like a sheep separated from its herd. As for Dan, yes, it would be better if she went to Eugene, wherever that was. Her sense of direction had abandoned her, but her usually reliable intuition alerted her that her presence was disturbing to Henrietta, and more so, to Jasper. What had Dan told them about her? Or hadn't told them? Her discomfort was growing, and she had not experienced any real sensation of welcome.

She was beginning to understand American roads and directions better. Finding Dan's apartment was fairly easy after New York, Chicago, and San Francisco. After the false start in Redding, maybe things will start coming into focus. She liked the idea of being close to a University. Maybe she could enroll in an English class to acquaint herself with American speech patterns, some of which continued to mystify her.

Madelaine was about to experience one of the rudest shocks of her life. For reasons that she could not have explained in any reasonable way, she did not knock on Dan's door right away. Instead twice she walked around the block, hesitant, almost afraid to see a man whose face she had trouble remembering. A year was a long time for two young adults. She had to remind herself that Dan was her husband but not yet her lover. They were married on paper but there had been no intimacy to bond them. And what little they remembered, at least what she remembered of him, belonged to another context. In France he was the handsome, uniformed Captain Dan Stokes; in California, the diminutive told a different story: he had reverted to Danny Stokes. It was as though the man she married had evaporated. She had looked up to the Captain. Would she now look down on

Danny? She was not sure she would have anything in common with Danny, a college freshman. How could a Captain become a freshman? Madelaine did not think of herself as a snob. There was no need to. She accepted class differences and social position as unquestioningly as she accepted eye color or stature. All her doubts came down to one as she circled the block. Who was the man behind the closed doors down the street?

On the last turn about the block Danny seemed to answer her question when he came out of the apartment with a girl on his arm. From her look and gestures Madelaine knew intuitively they had been intimate.

Embarrassment was etched in Danny's features, and he was too unsophisticated to conceal it. He was at a loss, unlike his companion who looked at her rival with a contemptuous smile.

"Madelaine," he blurted, "I didn't expect you today. Alice, this is Madelaine, my wife. She's French. Uh, Madelaine, meet Alice, she's my classmate in accounting. We were working on some problems together. Class problems. The class is hard."

Madelaine bowed slightly, while Alice gave her a miniature wave of the hand. Neither woman made a move toward the other.

"Uh, Alice, I'll see you in class. See if you can work out that last problem, will you?"

Alice delayed a few seconds, then nodded and said, "Will do. See you tomorrow, Danny. See you later, Mrs. Stokes," she said with a certain deliberate emphasis on 'Mrs.' "Bye now," she added as she sauntered off.

Madelaine was not yet familiar with some nuances of American English, but she recognized in Alice's tone the timeless scorn and challenge that one woman directs toward a rival.

Madelaine felt no jealousy, only shock and disillusionment. She had never loved Danny to begin with. Although she had not said so in words, hers was a *mariage de convenance,* a convenience her father had urged partly in order to save her from possible abuse and suffering, but mostly to make her another man's problem. She had read somewhere—was it in Rochefoucauld?—that good intentions commonly pave the road to evil results. For the first time in that revelatory moment, the full shabbiness of her circumstances became obvious to her. Too late she knew she had missed the chance to reject the arrangement and alter her destiny. Not that there was anything new in the agreement itself; arranged marriages were as old as human history. But normally, despite the frequent disregard for any feelings she might have for or against, the woman was a prize, a reward, or indemnification of some kind, perhaps a pawn in the game of statecraft. In a word, the woman in question was valuable, if not as a woman or a person, at least as a symbol or a solution. In her case, she saw that just as Danny's military glory had passed, so had the infatuation with his unwanted French bride. A year was an eternity for an immature man like Danny. What he rushed to call love had been a momentary hormonal effervescence, as quickly come and gone as the day of deliverance in Rouen. Now, out of her element and he firmly back in his, she was a stranger, an intruder, an embarrassment to all, and most of all, to herself. Danny was once again reduced to himself: a plain man of no exceptional qualities or ambitions. It was enough for him to rise once, once to act heroically; now he was back on the solid ground that was the sum and substance of his ambitions.

Though she did not and could not love the boy to which Dan had reverted, she longed for a man so strong that she could at least love his strength, if not him. In his prime, her father had been such a man, and such he remained until age and the Germans singled him out to rob him of his social standing and destabilize the family. In Danny's case, his strength was never more than an image created in her imagination. She longed in that instant for the man who for a shining moment had been Captain Dan but could not be again.

But she had no other options and moved into Danny's apartment. Neither she nor Danny mentioned Alice again, which meant that she was destined to remain their foremost marital problem. Madelaine quietly disposed of some intimate things Alice had left under the bed. Despite her disappointment with Danny, she worried that he might truly be in love with the girl. It would be easier if the items belonged to yet another girl, for it would be proof that he had only sexual liaisons and not emotional ties to a single woman. She was not yet familiar enough with his face to read his emotional language, but she had decided she would not stand in his way if Alice was his love and not simply his lover. It was not a willingness to sacrifice herself, for she had no emotional stake in their marriage to begin with. If it came to a separation, she did not know where she would go or what she would do, but she was sure the solution would present itself. It was not yet time to act and thus not the time to worry.

She was now fully aware that the uniformed Captain Dan was more of a uniform than a real person, and she reproached herself for being too gullible to make the distinction. The Americans had been an impressive, superior army with hierarchies and levels of command, but dissolved again into individuals and descended to a common democratic level she had not seen in European democracies. The Americans had never been anything else, but the Europeans had been feudal lords and peasants, crusaders, aristocrats, and monarchists with a thousand rivalries and intrigues. And who they had been, so in part they continued to be regardless of modern democratic overlays. It lent them a complexity lacking in the American character that could not be improvised. Even in its most sophisticated and intellectually accomplished forms, the American psyche was woven from a single democratic fiber, and though it simplified them, it also gave them a singular unity and strength. They could have a thousand nuances in their theology but in their social and political life, the two varieties were like opposite sides of the same coin. In the most benign sense she could give the word, she realized that she was among civil barbarians with great will and simple concepts. But here she was and though she dreaded going forward, there was no going back.

Two nights later, she gave herself to Danny, who delighted that she bled. She understood his male vanity but detested his crude delight in the time-honored proof of her virginity. For days following he was insatiable, and Madelaine was in misery not only because of his constant personal nearness but also because of nearly unbearable physical pain. She recalled a phrase from Choderlos de LaClos' *Liaisons dangereuses* that had always horrified her but which she could not erase from her memory: *"une certaine difficulté dans la marche"* (a certain difficulty in walking).

For her it was an unforgivable breach of the matrimonial secret that he told his father of her virginal status on their first visit to Redding. Jasper made a sly reference to it later and gave her a look that was not fatherly. From that moment Madelaine knew he was not a man to be trusted and was careful not to be alone with him.

Danny was progressing modestly in his studies. Adept at mathematics and capable in the sciences, he was dismal and disinterested in history, writing, and literature, unable to see any merit in topics that in his opinion had too much to do with Europe. He had seen all he wanted to see of the Old Continent and Madelaine could not instill an interest in him that he had rejected from the start and from the heart. She explained certain literary concepts to him, critiqued his writing as best her English permitted, and helped him get through the required courses in what for him was a mine field called humanities.

One day as she was returning from the library, she heard a piano in the Student Center. Just as she passed by, the pianist, a girl not much younger than Madelaine, did a couple of creditable glissandos and closed the keyboard. Madelaine smiled at her, and when the girl left the empty room, seated herself at the keyboard. A beloved Ravel composition, which she had not played in over a year, beckoned and she attacked it with an eagerness that was like hunger or a friendship long frustrated. In a moment, she was in an alternate universe, oblivious to all else. She was deep into the work and pleased that her fingers still retained much of their training when she noticed people around her. She stopped, embarrassed. Then her small public, half a dozen students and an older man, broke into spontaneous applause. She stood, bowed, and reached down to gather her purse and papers. The students smiled, congratulated her, and drifted away.

"No, miss, wait," said the gray-haired man who appeared to be around fifty. "I wish to talk to you."

"I did not mean to . . . I had no right."

"Miss, please, the piano is for all the students."

"But I am not a student, only the wife of one."

"That's not important," he said. "What matters is the music I have just heard coming from those tired and banged-up old keys. I am Dr. Klewzuski, of the Music Department and Professor of Piano. I have not heard your level of playing at this university since I left Prague six years ago. Who are you and where have you studied?" he said, holding out his hand to shake hers.

"I am Madelaine-Marie DuCordier-Stokes, sir," she responded in full formality as they shook hands. I studied with Professor Jacques LeFevre in Rouen and then two years at the Guildhall School in London with Professors Grassley and Goldstein. The War cut short my studies and I returned to France. Since then I have done no further studies."

"You are far advanced in your technique. I congratulate you. A talent like yours is rare in a place like this, too valuable not to be put to good use. Tell me, if you will, more about yourself."

The spent half an hour over coffee, and when Madelaine finally realized how much time had elapsed and rose to leave, they had agreed that she would play for the professorial staff the following Monday. "You may select the pieces. I would say two shorter works, including today's Ravel, if you like. I shall alert my colleagues. Do you have a piano available?"

"Sadly, no sir."

"Then you shall have access to mine in this room number and with this written permission if I am not readily available."

For the first time in months Madelaine was elated, but Danny was not.

"I hate to see you get bogged down with those humanists and musicians. There's no money and no future in any of that stuff. I was hoping you would sign up for courses in accounting."

"Danny, you have the talent for accounting. All I'm really suited for is music and the arts."

"What you're saying is that's all you're interested in. You don't care anything about me or what my interests are. You never back me in anything."

With that accusatory comment Danny was launched on his favorite tangent, one that invariably led to profanity, slammed doors, and hours away from home, driving from bar to bar. Madelaine knew it was useless to try to argue with him. So she went silent, the thing that irritated him most.

Regardless of Danny's pouting and profanity, she had no intention of yielding on this issue. Her conversation with Professor Klewzuski had inspired her to think that an opportunity of some kind might be possible for her. Her application for citizenship was proceeding smoothly and once she acquired full legal status, she might be able to put her talents to work and earn her own way. Without admitting it to herself, she was searching for a way to leave Danny and establish herself. It would be a favor to Danny. Without her, he could live his American life with a woman like Alice or her equivalent. That part would be no problem; physically, he was handsome.

Her trial recital, if it can be called that, was a small triumph. The professorial corps was duly impressed with her playing and her knowledge of musical literature. Professor Klewzuski recommended afterwards out of her hearing that Madelaine be hired as an adjunct professor, a perfect tutorial fit, he declared for their younger students, especially the young women, who could see in her accomplishments and talent what they aspired to achieve.

His recommendation was approved without dissension and after an administrative interview with the Dean and other officials, the offer was made, a one-semester appointment running from January through May. The salary was modest in the extreme, for which Professor Klewzuski apologized, but it was huge for Madelaine and she accepted it without hesitation.

Danny was furious when she told him, and if she judged correctly, a bit frightened by her sudden elevation. Now she allowed herself to think openly about a separation. She would bide her time and pray that everything would work for her and Danny. She wished him no harm, but he had so wounded her that she could not truthfully wish him anything else.

Then reality blindsided her. The next week she discovered she was pregnant. She thought of suicide and abortion, but besides being illegal, both were contrary to her religious heritage. She was not assiduous in her devotions but remained loyal to her heritage and took it as much for granted as the air she breathed.

Danny was bewildered by it all. When she told him, he drank at their small kitchen table, lamenting his impending fatherhood. It helped that despite not yet having his degree he had just been appointed Assistant Campus Director of Veterans Affairs mostly on the basis of his military rank and decorated service which restored some of his lost military prestige. Madelaine was too absorbed in her own tortured twist of fortune to care deeply one way or another about his circumstances.

That Friday he made his excuses and went out to celebrate both events with his friends, or so he said. He did not return. At three in the morning two officers from the Eugene police force knocked on the door and informed her that Danny had died in an automobile accident along with another passenger.

"A woman?" she asked simply.

The officers looked at each other before answering. "Yes, ma'am," the older man admitted. "Alice Overton, according to her identification. She was alive but died before the ambulance could get her to the hospital. Was she a relative?"

"Not exactly," she answered, "but I knew her. And my husband?"

"I'm afraid he died instantaneously, ma'am."

"It's better that way, if he had to go."

"Yes, ma'am," he said arching an eyebrow at her unemotional, monotone response.

"What must I do now, officers? I am not familiar with American laws and requirements in such cases."

"You'll need to come to the morgue first thing in the morning to formally identify the body. Then burial arrangements will be your responsibility. We saw that his driver's license gave a Redding, California address. If he has family there, I would think that's where he'll be buried."

"Yes, of course, his parents live there."

Danny was buried in his captain's uniform. Luckily his features were not disfigured in the wreck and he looked handsome. For a moment Madelaine saw again the man she had admired in France. Perhaps this was the real Dan, and the other man Danny an inferior imitation. She remembered reading that "Death clarifies at once what a man was."

Dan was Jasper and Henrietta's only child and their grief was uncontrollable. Madelaine was sad but too honest to feign a grief that she did not really feel for Danny. Nor was she close enough to Jasper and Henrietta to share their suffering. But simple human compassion moved her to tell them in a private moment that she was carrying his child. It was a light in their darkness. Jasper and Henrietta immediately urged Madelaine to move in with them, but she pleaded her contract to teach piano until June. Then they could decide, though to herself she swore that it would never happen if she could find the means to support herself in Eugene. No one mentioned the woman who died with Danny, but both she and his parents knew that it would feed the gossip mill for days to come.

Danny's accounts contained more money than she thought, for it turned out that he had concealed a checking account from her. His automobile was a total loss, but insurance would issue her a modest check for the Chevrolet. It was not much but with her university income it was enough. It was a start, the beginning of the rest of her life.

Time moved on; Jennifer was born in September. Henrietta preferred a family name for her granddaughter, but Madelaine found it hard to pronounce and overrode her mother-in-law's choice. Her university assignment was a triumph and Professor Klewzuski happily informed her that, allowing a semester off to recuperate and care for her baby, she would be contracted for the spring semester. She accepted, relieved that the unhappy prospect of having to live in Redding no longer tormented her. The Stokes took every occasion to visit Jennifer and doted doubly on her, now that Danny was gone. But Madelaine limited their visits and only rarely took Jennifer to Redding.

She was becoming known and beloved on campus. She had endured long erosions of spirit but was still more than anyone could see. Nor did she know herself her own depth. She projected a persona of laughter, gaiety, and above a gift of enchantment. Life had pushed her into contention in a setting that if at first was strange and uninviting, now became a world she could conquer but perhaps never come to love completely.

A regal side of her character began to emerge. She had come to America young, defensive and inexperienced. Now, even though she could be benevolent and generous, she was becoming a deliberate, directed woman whose still vigorous fancies were not allowed to stray into public view. She had matured away from her native land, and like transplanted exotic plants was growing into a new species. She could not judge how much of her unfolding character was due to her new setting or to her truncated heritage. Nor did she know of a sure way to determine if she was intellectually superior, as her growing circle of friends and admirers believed, or simply had the advantage of centuries of accumulated culture.

She imagined a phantom life back in France, then wondered how much she deviated from her alter ego abandoned in old Rouen. She always thought she would return some day, but after receiving word that her parents had died, and her brothers had managed to cut her out of the family inheritance, she was more comfortable with her American uncertainties than with any vestiges of her childhood world. She told herself that she could rise above resentments, but she was not convinced and was unwilling to put herself to the test.

Her beauty was enticing, and every man believed, or at least hoped, that her charms were meant for him. But she was in no rush to engage herself with another man; her first love was Jennifer. She taught her all she knew of art, music, literature, and language. And Jennifer was compliant, a perfect complement to her mother, though taller and proportioned like an American girl, reflecting her father's genetic heritage.

She took lovers after a few years but never with the intention of marrying again. To her, marriage was like a cancer she had survived; it was gone but the horror remained. The first lover was a widowed university colleague, a kind, gentle, unassertive man who loved her with a devotion honed and perfected in two dozen years of happy matrimony. Her passion in lovemaking startled him, causing him to think he had masculine powers he had never suspected. He was never to know the passion came not from him but was an eruption of her repressed self. He longed for conventional marriage, which allowed her to drop him without any lingering sentimentality.

She was kind to her men, especially to a young Frenchman emotionally lost, as she once was, in prototypical America. She abandoned him when it became apparent to her that he would never transition to a higher plane. "Go back to France," she told him, "and find yourself a French wife. It's what you need and where you belong." Without exception, the men believed in childlike innocence that her kindness was proof of their manhood. None satisfied her innermost need, which was her longing for a superman. She had not lost her youthful, unrealistic ideal of a primal hero who would take what he wanted and yet return her love quadrupled with desire, lust, and the tenderness of true power and mastery of all he surveyed. It was unrealistic, and she knew it better than anyone could have told her. The hope was paradoxically impossible, for it was the image of a giant who embodied Descartes, Pascal, and Wagnerian power.

Madelaine became a popular fixture at the University as Jennifer grew into womanhood. She studied art history at Berkeley, became a museum curator, a wife, and the mother of two daughters, Marie and Olivia. In marriage she was only marginally more successful than Madelaine, and after a dozen years husband Stanley Blackwell, a middle level executive for a shoe company, who drifted through a series of infidelities and disappeared from her life, leaving barely a trace. No love was left, so none was lost. His daughters rarely mentioned his name.

Jennifer moved them to New York. The bond with Madelaine remained, but for the Marie and Olivia their grandmother became a celebrity event, not a daily familiarity. When they were fifteen and thirteen, Madelaine agreed at their urging to accompany them to France. Jennifer had been to Paris several times and knew better than her mother the post-war tempo of the country. For Madelaine it was a melancholy journey into memories. She did not miss France so much as she missed the person she could have been in her homeland. The phantom Madelaine whose image and imaginary life she had kept alive for many years had at last succumbed to time like an aged relative long since laid to rest.

Against her wishes, she yielded to their insistence that she return to Rouen. She recognized buildings and streets, yet they were strangely at odds with the large dimensions she remembered and the shrunken realities she found. She had returned but could not penetrate the city, and there were no close relatives to reacquaint her with her birthplace. Some places do not forgive us for abandoning them, she thought, and places are more alive and pliable than we think.

The jumble of impressions and ideas were meaningful to her but would have been nonsensical to Jennifer and her granddaughters. The young may dream and say what they please no matter how preposterous, she thought without any hint of bitterness; but on pain of being suspected of mental decline, the elderly must stay within the boundaries of simple rationality and limited sentimentality. It was simply a fact that she had no intention of denying.

Her musical peak came at fifty when she gave a series of concerts in California and Oregon that earned favorable reviews. She dismissed most of the accolades with her private assessment that most of them were the praise of unmusical mediocrities pressed into artistic service for want of qualified critics. She hoped for delayed recognition before larger and more appreciative publics.

It never came. At sixty arthritis was beginning to slow her hands and betray her in the midst of performances. And as her physical abilities waned, so did her enthusiasm for performance and teaching, though she dutifully carried on until she was nearly seventy. Only rarely did she agree to play the organ or piano at church and only in emergencies when the contracted musicians were ill or unavailable.

She commenced a general withdrawal from the world, putting more distance between her busy life and ideal inner horizons. There was a magic in horizons, she thought, for they divide the real world from possible realms that were calling her in ever stronger voices.

Each time it was harder to go back to the hard, heavy, ugly world. *Trop dur, trop lourd, trop laid* (too hard, too heavy, too ugly) she said, no longer in English to herself and sometimes not to other people. She was shedding English like a garment that was now passé and out of style. Each time she went further into a more promising universe, staying longer and turning back ever more reluctantly to the old one. On these excursions the dull horizon commenced to crack and chunks of it fall away, allowing her to see breathtakingly beautiful colors and music beyond. How could she go back? Or why? There was Jennifer and the grandchildren, of course, but she could be of no more use to them. And she did not want to be a burden or an embarrassment. She was tired of burdens and awkwardness and longed for gracefulness. Were it not for the errors and ugliness that crushed her maybe she could soar. She needed to soar and sing like a wounded, impatient lark whose wing has finally healed.

Further she ventured as the months and years passed, ever further, until one day she passed a point of no return. This time it was all right, the bright lights beyond the heavy darkness seemed to be saying to her, for lights have a language of their own. She could have returned; her will was still intact, but now she did not have to go back to the world that had been her familiar prison. This time she could go on, she had permission from a high, indisputable source to go on and not to turn back, never again to turn back in sadness and responsibility to the relentless heaviness of the world. And the further she went, the more brilliant the colors became, the colors that harmonized as music, as love, as beauty, all the wonder she had sensed, and longed for all her life. Now she skipped and ran as the heaviness dropped away, until finally beyond the flimsy real boundaries and unreasonable limits of the city she stood at the shore of an immense sea and delighted again after her earthly exile in the wonder of endless creation. It was breathtakingly new, but also immensely ancient, and she realized she had known it somewhere in another time and another place. It was the destiny and destination she had always yearned for. And there was no darkness in it. Now, finally, she felt light enough to soar.

*****

"Ladies, where did you find Professor Stokes?" Dr. Holcombe asked Hazel Phillips and Lou Ann Bridges.

"Can you believe it, Doctor?" Hazel said. "The poor thing was down in the city park, probably been there all night and barefoot in this frost. She had taken her shoes off. We were taking our morning walk and saw her lying there in the grass."

"And getting pneumonia in the process. Does anyone have a number for her daughter? She needs to get here right away. I am not hopeful we can save her."

"I have her number at home, Doctor. Madelaine gave it to me last year when she was sick."

Hazel stayed in the waiting room while Lou Ann ran home to call Jennifer. By the time she returned, Madelaine had slipped away. .

"Poor demented thing," Hazel said, shaking her head. "I guess her mind and body just quit completely on her this time. We all knew she was slipping these last two or three years and that it was only a matter of time."

"Yes, but you know something, Hazel? She never lost her music. She complained of arthritic hands, but you couldn't tell it by the way she played. She could still do magic with Debussy, Ravel, Grieg, Beethoven, Tchaikovsky, Rachmaninov, and the other great composers. She knew them all like old friends. How could she do that with her mind practically gone?"

"It's a mystery to me too, Lou Ann. I say this as someone who can't carry a decent tune, as you well know, but when it's all said and done, maybe the music we make of our life is all any of us have left at the end to give back to the Creator."

Honorable Mention

Saturday, April 14, 1956

The arsonist responsible for the fire that destroyed the landmark Carlisle mansion and severely injured owner Wesley ("Wes") Carlisle sensationalized the county. Sheriff Thurman Rogers, trailing in a tight reelection campaign against Constable Troy Runnells, was anxious to make an arrest in the case and tip the odds in his favor.

"Now that we have an eyewitness to the crime, we've got the evidence we need to arrest Kearney Patterson for arson, and if Mr. Carlisle dies, homicide to boot," he told deputies Howard Maddox and Jimmie Lee Craft. "So you two get your butts out there to the Gilmore farm and bring him in. And no screwups, you hear? If he gets away, I'll hang both your hides out to dry on a barbed-wire fence. You understand me?"

They mumbled their assent but resented having to work past their normal shift time. Probably it would mean missing several innings of the big game against Valley High on a night when Howard's son Jerry was pitching, and Jimmie Lee's heavy-hitting son Bobby was featured at first base. Both men, especially Howard, were ready to take it out on Kearney if he gave them any trouble.

Thirty minutes later, Howard and Jimmie Lee waited as the big John Deere tractor chugged dustily toward them, its hungry disks chewing the remaining sliver of unplowed acreage. Then with drawn weapons, they ordered Kearney, 22, off the tractor, arrested and handcuffed him, and with patrol car sirens shrieking and red lights flashing, hauled him away to the Carlisle County jail.

Kearney asked them for time to tell Harvey Gilmore, land and tractor owner, what had happened. But the deputies denied both requests.

"We got better things to do, Patterson," Howard reminded him. "Best thing you can do is to sit back there and keep your trap shut. You got that?"

Kearney didn't answer.

"I asked you if you heard what I said, and you better answer me when I ask you something."

"I heard you—both times."

Jimmie Lee saw danger signs as Howard's hair-trigger temper reddened his broad face. He knew from experience that his partner was not above brutalizing prisoners.

"Hey, Howard, we got him in custody, and that's the main thing. Let's just get him on to jail as quick as we can so we can get to the game and watch our boys play."

"Yeah, okay, just as long as he don't smart off with me. But if he spouts off again—"

Howard left the implied threat hanging.

Not only did circumstantial evidence point to Kearney—the proximity of his place to the Carlisle estate, an empty gas can in his '46 Ford truck bed—but much more damning was Bennie McCann's claim that he had seen Kearney slipping around the mansion not long before it burned to the ground. Besides, everybody knew that based on Bennie's eyewitness testimony the year before, Kearney had served two months in the county jail for burning one of the Carlisle estate barns.

"So, Patterson, you couldn't leave bad enough alone, could you? You know something? You are a real pain in the ass for this county. But this is the worst yet: arson and maybe a charge of homicide. Open and shut case. Bennie McCann's eyewitness testimony will nail you to the wall," Rogers said, shaking his head as Howard shoved Kearney into the cell and locked the door. "You'll be lucky if Mr. Carlisle survives his injuries, otherwise, they may fry your ass in the chair. But even if they don't, you'll spend some serious time in prison. The two months you were my guest here in the county jail last year won't compare to what you'll go through down in State Prison."

"I wasn't guilty then and I'm not guilty now. Bennie McCann lied the first time and he's lying again if he says he saw me around the Carlisle mansion when it burned down. I wasn't even in Carlisle County last Thursday, and not last year either."

"Um-hum, so you say. Well, a court of law found you guilty the first time, and this time around the evidence against you is even stronger. Seems like you have a habit of setting things on fire. I don't know what you've got against Wes Carlisle, but whatever it is, you burned his barn and now his house and left him at the point of death. What you got to say about that?"

"Nothing that would do any good at the moment, Sheriff. But I do ask a favor of you."

"A favor? Doing favors for prisoners is not our business. But what is it?"

"Well, two things actually. I need to get word to Mr. Gilmore about his tractor. I had to leave it out in the field instead of driving it back to the shed. And the other thing is, I have my horse stabled at my place. If Mr. Gilmore or somebody doesn't get out there to turn him loose in the pasture to graze and get water, he won't last long. I hate to think of him suffering."

"We'll do it for Mr. Gilmore and the horse, not for you Patterson."

Meanwhile, the deputies hurried out to the patrol car. Ignoring protocol by switching on the siren and police lights at red lights and stop signs to clear the traffic, Howard got them to the stadium by the second inning, just in time to see Carlisle High score three runs against Valley on Bobby's Craft's fifteenth home run.

Doctors shook their heads when asked about Wes Carlisle's chances for recovery, but he fought for life for nearly three months despite severe burns and compromised lungs. Since the charges against Kearney did not yet involve a homicide, with Harvey Gilmore's help he was able to make bail, finish spring planting, and attend to other matters before his trial docketed for the fall.

Kearney had no illusions about his chances in court. The Carlisle name was iconic. As the last of his pioneer family line for whom both the county and town were named, bachelor Carlisle was not only the county's biggest landholder but a living link to its proud past. Consequently, by near-unanimous consensus the public prejudged Kearney guilty of a cowardly act that injured an outstanding man who had served the county and state in several high offices without a hint of scandal in any of them. No, Kearney knew he could expect nothing less than the full tonnage of the law to come crashing down on him.

At the first church service after his three-day jail time, the congregation either shunned him or made awkward efforts to be cordial. Other acquaintances suddenly acted like strangers in his presence, choosing to avoid his pew and eye contact if he happened by. Even old high school classmates had better things to do than talk to him. He had experienced it all before except the biggest jolt that happened when Alice Burk, 20, stopped by his pew to give him a small box and a terse explanation.

"Kearney, here's your high school ring back. I believed you the first time, but not now. Bennie saw you do it. So don't call me or come around anymore. We're done."

After church he saw Alice and Bennie drive off in his new Chevrolet. That tells me a lot, he thought. Bennie's been after her since high school. He tossed the little box in a trash can and tried to slip the ring back on his finger, but it was too small. I guess I've outgrown it, and maybe in more ways than one, come to think of it. Well, that's that.

That afternoon he set up his easel, got out his oils and brushes, and commenced a new painting. For hours the ideal world of his art was an island of peace in a sea of grimness. He had inherited an artistic talent from his mother which he expressed in panoramic landscapes and farm scenes. One hung in the county courthouse until it was taken down after his first arrest. He knew Harvey and Dorothy Gilmore still displayed theirs. The fate of others in local homes was unknown.

Kearney attended church the next two Sundays, but things were no better. He tried to tune out Preacher Orville Richter's veiled references to him, recalling instead scriptural exhortations to avoid being a stumbling block to other believers. He had promised his mother on her deathbed that he would remain faithful to God and Church. But now he felt he must suspend the second part of the vow so as not to be a spiritual hindrance to others. He would read his Bible and say his prayers in private, as he promised, hoping she would understand. His mother had spent her own life largely estranged from people. Now Kearney seemed headed in the same direction.

Under the turmoil he tried to remember his father, but the memories were distorted images adrift in the infinite, timeless world of childhood. Vaguely he recalled the strange man he called father who would come home on weekends from a far-off city, perhaps St. Louis, or was it somewhere called Kansas City? He seemed impossibly large to Kearney. Sometimes he would bring home candy and presents, but Kearney was too timid to speak in his presence. The man talked a lot, too much, Kearney thought. He was not used to listening to so many words at once. Silent, soothing reading words were the best kind, his mother's kind, not the noisy, conflictive ones the man spoke.

Then even those memories ceased. He remembered when he was six or seven being in a church with unsmiling people dressed in black; then the scene shifted outside to a grassy knoll his mother called a cemetery where a large wooden box was being let down into the ground by ropes as a robed man said words he did not understand. A casket, his mother said when he asked.

"What's a casket, Momma?" he asked.

She did not answer.

"Momma, can I run up the hill?"

"No, Kearney. This is a cemetery. It's not for playing."

"But why? It needs to be played in. It's so pretty and flowery."

She did not answer.

He knew very little about his mother. She rarely spoke and seldom smiled. Once, though—maybe it was on that same strange day—she smiled and told him about a doll she had when she was little.

"Her name was Cynthia."

"What happened to Cynthia, Momma?"

She did not answer.

"Do you still have her?"

"My Aunt hid her from me."

"Why? Cynthia was your doll, wasn't she?"

"My Aunt was afraid I would wear her out. She liked to save things for a proper time."

"Did you ever find Cynthia again?"

"When I was grown, in my Aunt's old trunk after she died."

"Did you play with Cynthia again?"

"No."

"Why, Momma?"

"I was too old by then."

"Can't grown-up people play, Momma?"

"Some try but none should."

"Why, Momma?"

"Playing is for children."

"Have you ever tried, Momma?"

She did not answer but gave him a rare smile, went to her room, and closed the door.

Widow Cora Patterson was devoted to the church and spent hours each day reading the Bible. She had no close friends or family and told him very little about herself or her relatives. Occasionally she exchanged visits with Mrs. Dorothy Gilmore, who admired her exquisite needlework and often commissioned her for sewing projects and dressmaking for herself and her teenage daughter Becky. Mrs. Gilmore was embarrassed to pay her so little for her work, but Cora would accept only a modest compensation, politely but firmly rejecting anything over a bare modicum. Near the mortal end of her final illness, she presented gifts to Dorothy and Becky: a beautifully knitted blue sweater for Becky's senior year in high school and artistically detailed place settings for Mrs. Gilmore's table.

"Oh my goodness, Cora, they're astonishingly beautiful!" Dorothy gushed. "But you shouldn't have, not with your health in question."

"It's my way of thanking you for being so good to Kearney and me. May God bless you and your family for your many kindnesses over the years."

A week later she died in her sleep, "the death of the just," Mrs. Gilmore described her passing. She took many secrets with her, one of which at first seemed to seal Kearney's fate but later proved to be the key to his deliverance.

He missed her silent presence because it had matched and balanced his own, but in time his solitude expanded to fill the void. Since his life had never been defined by happiness, he had no reason now to define it by grief.

People wondered how a single man barely past twenty would—or could—manage the forty-acre farm bordered on the east side by the vast Carlisle estate. Soon after his mother's death, several prospective buyers approached him with by-out offers, but Kearney had no interest in selling. The place was paid for, had a two-acre lake of good water, fencing and pasture; a good barn, a fifteen-acre stand of prime timber, and a solid four-room house. Perched atop Penn Mountain—the exaggerated name of the highest promontory around—it offered a pleasant panorama of the surrounding countryside, which he loved to sketch and paint. No, thank you, Kearney told each prospective buyer. I'll keep it.

In fact, he had run, or at least maintained, the place since he was thirteen. Years earlier, his mother had leased the water rights annually to cattleman Henry Gilmore and the tillable land on a similar lease to his farmer brother Harvey. The double lease income was modest, but Kearney's earnings in Harvey's employ increased as he acquired the strength and skills of manhood. The total was enough for them.

Though very different in character, talkative, outgoing Harvey developed a genuine affection for lean, inwardly turned Kearney. Their relationship survived both Kearney's first arrest a year earlier and pending trial for the Carlisle conflagration.

It bothered Dorothy Gilmore to learn that Kearney no longer attended church. Knowing how much it meant to his mother, she brought it up with Harvey.

"Harvey, it troubles me to learn that Kearney doesn't attend church anymore. You know how devoted Cora was."

"Well, honey, I can't say I blame Kearney for leaving, not after the way those hypocrites treated him."

"Harvey, don't call them that. There are good Christians in that church, including some of our neighbors."

"I guess you're right, honey, but I could do without that preacher of theirs, that Orville Richter. Good men tell me you can't trust him when it comes to business. Won't pay his debts, so they say. And I get mad as hell at the way this whole damned county has already judged Kearney. And a lot of it is because Rogers and that lying Bennie McCann have been stirring up talk against the boy. I just know in my heart that Kearney didn't burn that barn last year, much less the Carlisle mansion this time around. I hope Runnells beats the tar out of Rogers in this next election. We need better law enforcement than what we've got right now in this county. And in my opinion our court system doesn't pass the smell test. Anyway, you know how I feel about Kearney. I wish I could help him, but I don't know what else I can do. I did what I could by helping him get out on bail."

"There may be one thing we can do for him in another way."

"And what would that be?"

"Maybe we could talk him into going to our church. Saints or sinners, we are supposed to welcome people into our congregation, aren't we?"

"Honey, you know I can't argue with you on that point. So what do you have in mind?"

"I would like for all of us to go up to his house and talk to him, invite him to our church. I could drive up there by myself, but I think it's better if we all go."

"Becky too?"

"I talked to her about it. She would rather go to a party her friend Faye is giving tonight. But she'll go if I insist. She and Kearney are not close friends, but it would be good for him to be around somebody near his age."

"Could just the two of you go see him? Or maybe you could just talk to him on the telephone. He had one put in last year after his mother got sick. I'm up to my eyeballs in work, now that Kearney has taken time off to get his stuff in order before the trial."

"I think Kearney would listen more to you than to us. And it has to be in person. You're the closest thing he has to a father. Besides, it's getting cloudy and I don't want just the two of us driving that road up there in case the weather turns bad. I want my big strong husband to go with me."

"Honey, you lead me around like a trained bear, but I wouldn't have it any other way. You know that. So when do you want to go?"

"What's wrong with today? It's already getting late, but Kearney is in a precarious position. If Wes Carlisle dies, God forbid, Kearney's bail gets revoked, as I understand it, and he lands right back in jail. Becky and I will be ready in half an hour."

She looked Harvey up and down. "And you need to put on some better pants and a good shirt."

"I don't see why, if we're just going up to see Kearney. He won't care. He sees me like this all the time. Besides your and Becky's good looks will more than make up for my ugly."

"Harvey Gilmore, don't think you can flatter your way out of this. I don't want you going anywhere off this farm dressed like that."

"I know what you're thinking. What if something happens and I end up in the hospital, right?"

"I wasn't thinking anything of the sort. But the way you dress is a reflection on me. Even if you are my trained bear as you say, my dear, you still need to practice so you don't forget."

Becky grumbled a bit, Harvey changed clothes, Dorothy retouched her hair, and the three of them drove up to Kearney's house late in the day. He was surprised but relieved to see them. Word about Wes Carlisle's condition was not promising, and he kept an eye on the road, fearful that the black patrol car might show up at any time to pick him up on an added charge of homicide.

Dorothy was surprised and pleased by how neat the house was. Cora had been a meticulous housekeeper, but Kearney was a man, and she knew from experience that men and mess usually go together like filth under fingernails. Dorothy shuddered to think what her own house would look like if it were left in

Harvey's care. They were especially impressed by the reverent placement of Cora's King James Bible on a small table draped by a blue velvet covering with accompanying miniature ivory angels. After a few minutes of conversation, the Bible arrangement segued smoothly into the reason for their visit.

Kearney listened politely, expressed some reservations about switching to a different denomination, but then accepted their invitation to attend Good Hope Church.

"You know how much Momma respected you folks. She always said that you lived your faith. And I say so too. My only concern is that other folks may not be happy to have me around, and the last thing I want is to cause you folks trouble, not after all you have done for us, for me."

Thunder was coming closer. Huge drops of rain were lifting puffs of dust in the yard and streaking the windshield of Harvey's Chevrolet pickup.

"It looks like Mother Nature has got some rough stuff on her mind tonight," Harvey remarked as a lightning flash illuminated the room. "Kearney, I think we better get going before things get worse. We'll meet you at church Sunday morning."

They pulled out of the yard and headed down the mountain. The lightning was coming quicker now with blinding sheets of rain. Thunder shook the frame house. Suddenly car lights flashed across the window where Kearney was standing. The Sheriff's patrol, he thought in alarm. But no; it was the Gilmore's, drenched and dripping as they rushed in from the deluge.

"Man alive! We almost bought it!" Harvey said.

"What happened?" Kearney asked.

"We got about a quarter of a mile down the road when lightning struck that big Red Oak by the gate and it fell across the road. There was no way to get around it. We're lucky it didn't fall across the truck. If it had . . ."

"But that road is narrow with ditches and there's no place to turn around. How in the world did you make it back up here to the house?"

"The only way I could, in reverse gear all the way, and raining so hard I could barely see the road. I guess the Lord guided us because I couldn't really tell where I was going. I don't think I've ever seen heavier rain."

"But you got us back safely, dear," Dorothy said as her panic began to subside. "Now you see why I wanted you to drive us up here. Just think if Becky and I had been alone."

"Oh, Momma, I don't even want to think about it!" Becky said, shivering from the thought and the rain.

"But now you're all here safe under my roof, humble as it is. Let me see, I have some blankets and quilts in the hall closet. And lots of old cloths in the back room. Let me start digging them out. First thing, you have to get out of those wet clothes and get warmed up. And don't even think of trying to drive home tonight. That road will be a creek until the water has time to run off. I have beds and food, and if the blankets and things aren't enough, I can build a fire in the fireplace. Let me put it this way: this house is yours for as long as you need it—and as long as you like."

For an hour the rain, thunder, and lightning continued in Noachian fury. Then reluctantly it began to recede toward the northern horizon. By then everybody was dry and outfitted in outlandish combinations of colors and sizes, while Dorothy, expert and resourceful cook that she was, started searching for the makings of dinner. After the inventory she scolded Kearney.

"Kearney, I see why you're so thin. I can tell by your pantry and refrigerator that you eat like a bird. As hard as you work, you need more nourishment. I know for a fact that your mother was an excellent cook, and it pains me to think that this son of hers goes around half starved."

He laughed and explained: "I didn't inherit what I guess you could call her culinary talent. I just sort of toss whatever's handy in the pot. You don't want to know how some of it turns out. But it keeps me going."

Harvey was about to comment about how Kearney needed a wife, but untypically for him, thought better of it with Becky present and began wondering about clearing the fallen red oak.

"But Kearney, you may not know—or care—how to cook, but you did inherit some of your mother's artistic talent," Becky exclaimed. "I don't remember seeing this landscape painting before. It's similar to the one we have at home, but to be honest, I like this one better. It's really good."

"Thank you. It was Momma's favorite too. That's why she hung it in this room where she spent most of her time. It was accepted last year for the state exhibition and got an "Honorable Mention."

"That's where you were when Bennie McCann claimed he saw you prowling around Wes Carlisle's barn, isn't it?" Harvey commented.

"Yessir, they took my picture with two of the judges and gave me a signed and dated certificate. I gave it to Momma when I got home. She was proud of it, as I was, but I don't know where she put it. I've turned this house upside down looking for it. But no luck, and without it, I couldn't prove my whereabouts the day that barn burned."

"But you told the court about it as I remember," Harvey said.

"Yessir, but they claimed they had looked into it and found nothing."

"You know what that means, don't you?" Harvey said leaning forward and tapping Kearney on the arm.

"No sir, just that I was puzzled they couldn't verify my presence at the state exhibition."

"It means they didn't check it out at all, if you want my opinion. You were a convenient victim, another miscarriage of justice that has become the rule, not the exception, in Carlisle County."

"What about this year?" Becky asked. "Did you submit anything?"

"I did, but my life has been such a mess since last year that I didn't really have anything that good. The painting I submitted was exhibited but didn't win anything."

"But do you have verification that you entered this year's competition?" she wanted to know.

"No, not really, only the original letter of invitation to exhibit my work. The nonwinners didn't receive anything after the show."

"But you were there, weren't you?"

"I was there until a little after 5 p.m. That's when we were allowed to pick up our paintings."

"Do you have any verification of that fact: motel, restaurant, service station receipts, anything that proves you were not in Carlisle County the day and evening the mansion burned?"

"All I have is a receipt from a filling station, but it doesn't have a date on it. I drove straight home after the show, got back around daylight the next morning."

"And probably didn't have anything to eat on the way," Dorothy called from the kitchen.

"Does that receipt have a number?" Becky asked.

"It does have a number."

"Then by jingo it has a date," Harvey said excitedly.

"I don't follow you."

"Simple. It's just a matter of checking the number series. That should tell you the day of the transaction regardless of whether or not the date was stamped on the receipt. But, Kearney, if push comes to shove in the mansion case, my best advice is not to tell the prosecution up front anything you don't have to, and don't turn over anything material—like the gas stub—to them, or it could just up and disappear, There's something crooked down at that courthouse. I'm convinced of it, and I'm not the only one that thinks so."

At that point Dorothy called them to dinner. It was the best food Kearney had tasted since his mother died.

After dinner, Kearney took a flashlight and went out to check the barn and the horse. All was fine. Not long afterwards, they settled down for the night: Dorothy and Harvey in the main bedroom, Becky in the adjacent room, and Kearney in the room off the kitchen. He fell asleep thinking of clearing the obstruction in the road and worked in his dreams to clear the obstructions in his life.

All were up early the next day: a sparklingly clear morning without a cloud in the sky. Dorothy and Becky managed to scrounge up breakfast with the odds and ends left in Kearney's meager larder. Then he and Harvey took axes, wedges, a crosscut saw, and a bottle of kerosene to degum the saw teeth and headed off to attack the red oak. As they were leaving, Becky came out to ask a favor of Kearney.

"Kearney, would you mind if I take your landscape down to get a better look at it in daylight? I have an art class in school, and next week we'll be working on perspectives, and I need some ideas. I promise I'll be careful with it."

"Be my guest, Becky, but remember I'm strictly an amateur with no professional training. They didn't even offer art back when I was in high school. I'm like a Grandma Moses."

"Well, you're way ahead of me."

Half an hour later before they had made a real dent in the tree trunk, Becky came running, waving a paper.

"Kearney! Kearney! I found it! The certification," she gasped. "It was wedged behind picture frame. That's where Mrs. Patterson put it. And there's a photograph of you and the judges you mentioned. It must have been there all the time!"

Kearney slapped his head for stupidity. "Of course, right where I should have looked to start with! Why of course! Why didn't I think of that? It makes sense. Becky, you're an angel! You may have just saved my life!"

"No, Kearney, I didn't do anything. It just fell out by accident. Otherwise, I might not have even noticed it was there. But I'm glad because I know it's important to you."

"Sweetie," Harvey corrected her as he wiped sweat from his forehead, "don't be too sure. Sometimes what we call accidents are strings being pulled by higher powers. Just think: the storm came at its appointed time, the tree fell just when it was supposed to, and because of these things, you just happened to be there to find the papers. It all happened as we used to say, 'accidentally on purpose', a purpose way above our understanding. But now, Kearney, remember what I told you: hang on to those papers with your life. You may need them soon."

"Harvey, Becky, I'll take the advice, but now that I think about it. I can't personally hang on to the evidence, and I don't want to leave it in the house. Prisoners have to turn over all their stuff at lockup, and who knows if it gets returned if things are like you say they are, Harvey. And houses get burned, don't they? So what if I leave the documents with you? They're safer with you than with me."

"Smart thinking," Harvey said approvingly. "I promise you we'll take care of them, won't we, sweetie?"

"You can count on it, Kearney. After all, I feel like I have a stake in all this now."

They finished sawing through the massive tree trunk and rolled the blocking section out of the roadway. The water runoff was nearly complete by midday, and the Gilmores left soon after, reaffirming the plan to meet on Sunday.

The meeting was delayed. Later that same afternoon the dreaded black patrol car drove up and deputies Howard and Jimmie Lee took Kearney into custody. Wes Carlisle had died during the storm and bail was automatically revoked. Kearney spent the next two months in jail. In September his trail began.

As Sheriff Rogers said months earlier, it appeared to be an open and shut case against Kearny. Rogers was beaming now that political momentum had swung back in his favor. And a guilty verdict would seal the deal for his third term. He scoffed when defense attorney Carlson Kilgore promised Judge Sidney Shavers and jury that he would show that his client was not in the county when the arsonist or arsonists burned the Carlisle mansion and caused the eventual death of Mr. Wesley Carlisle.

The first two days of the trial were consumed largely with

legal preliminaries and skirmishes as each side sized up the opposition and honed its arguments. Only on the third day did the legal war begin in earnest. Bennie McCann, key witness in the prosecution's case, convincingly told in his own words how he observed Kearney Edward Patterson wearing a familiar red jacket approach the Carlisle mansion, gas can in hand, and splash walls and shrubbery with gasoline. An objection was raised: witness could not ascertain the nature of the liquid in the can. Objection sustained. Witness will refrain from offering conjectures and confine himself to facts. How was the witness able to describe the jacket as being red if it was night? Witness responded that he saw it was red when the accused walked under a lighted portion of the grounds. In end the witness seemed credible.

But not to Kilgore. He had a sixth sense about witness testimony, and he knew Bennie was lying. He was the lynchpin in the prosecution's case but the weak link for Kilgore, and he had taken down better liars than Bennie. Now the trap was set and tomorrow he would spring it. People wondered how Kearney Patterson had been able to hire a lawyer famed for his brilliant courtroom maneuvers. But in this one, the local prosecutorial team declared he had overreached himself and was about to get nailed, they agreed gleefully. And they were eager to show him up. Kearney is as guilty as sin, but even if he isn't, our case is airtight. As far as the prosecution was concerned, a guilty verdict was vastly more important than actual guilt.

For the remainder of the day, things proceeded as they predicted. Kilgore offered only weak arguments on behalf of client Kearney: that he was not in the vicinity but at an art exhibition in a distant city at least ten hours driving time away.

The prosecution asked for proof. The eyewitness foundation of the case seemed invulnerable, and the defense appeared to be on life support.

Kilgore knew better. He had taken the case with a larger purpose than defending an innocent man. Kilgore was for justice, but he also suspected that there were bigger fish to be caught and an eventual reward that went far beyond Kearney. If he played this right, it could propel him into high office.

The next morning Kilgore sprang his trap. Recalling Bennie McCann to the stand, he pointed out that this was the second time Bennie claimed to witness his client in the commission of a felony. How convenient. Are we to assume, sir, that you make it your business to follow Mr. Patterson about? Immediate objection by the prosecution. Your honor, details of prior cases have no bearing in this one. Objection sustained. Confine your questioning to the facts under consideration, Mr. Kilgore. But doubts had been planted in the jurors' minds. Then came the clincher: Kilgore's assistant gave the prosecution copies of the certificate of Honorable Mention, duly dated and signed, as well as the gasoline stub duly ascertained to indicate a sale to the defendant the day the Carlisle mansion burned. A ripple of whispers ran through the assembly. Judge Shaver called for order. Kilgore attacked. Now, Mr. McCann, would you like to reconsider your testimony? I remind you that the punishment for perjury is severe, and by the evidence you have committed it on two occasions. "I thought it was him," Bennie offered, squirming on the stand. Objection, your honor. The defense is badgering the witness. Objection sustained. This line of questioning is out of place. But Kilgore was too astute to be baited by a biased judge. "I shall, as an officer of the court, defer to the jury to make that determination."

The prosecution was livid. Why wasn't this evidence, as the defense calls it, made available sooner to the prosecution as legal protocol requires? Kilgore replied calmly that he saw it for the first time only this morning, and as soon as he did, duly passed the information along to the prosecution. (It was the literal truth; as per his instruction he had not personally laid eyes on it earlier.) He had covered his rear and now had won the case. Cheers overwhelmed Judge Shaver's futile gavel when the jury declared Kearney innocent of both charges against him.

But as Kilgore foresaw, the heavier legal lifting now began. When a man of his reputation and wealth suggested that Carlisle County needed to be investigated for corruption, the State listened and moved in. Bennie broke down and confessed that his testimony had been bought and paid for. Is that how you, apparently without steady employment, were able to buy a new automobile? He confessed it so. Who paid you? He named names, and once a money trail was discovered, it led to others, one to Judge Shavers, another to a prominent law firm, still another to a Carlisle banker, and an out-of -state developer. Thurman Rogers lost the election, which meant that his chief deputies Howard and Jimmie Lee lost their jobs as well. Eventually a sordid plan emerged that tied all the nefarious activities together in a master plot to gain possession of the Carlisle property and perhaps demented old Wes's money as well. Now that the plot had been foiled speculation ran rampant about who would inherit the estate. But that is another story.

Through it all Kilgore proceeded methodically and astutely, pulling the right legislative and judicial strings, building public opinion in favor of hardworking, orphaned Kearney picked on and mistreated by powerful, corrupt forces and forced to serve time for a crime he did not commit and then as a crowning indignity brought to a travesty of a trial. He deserves indemnity, Kilgore argued publicly and effectively. Under State oversight, Carlisle County made a formal apology and shelled out $175,000 in restitution. Kearney was pleased to pay Kilgore $35,000 in fees. How could he hesitate between imprisonment—or worse--and freedom, his good name, and enough money to take control of his future. As for Kilgore, he was on his way to ever bigger and more lucrative legal battles.

Not long after the trial Kearney found a letter from Alice in his mailbox.

> *Dear Kearney:*
> *I guess you heard that I broke up with Bennie.*
> > *He turned out to be a crook and I never want to see him again.*
> *I am so sorry I treated you the way I did, and if*
> *I get a chance I would like to apologize in person.*
> *I wish you all the best.*
> > *LOVE*
> > *Alice*

Kearney counted the "I"s in her letter. Five lines and nine "I"s. That tells me a lot about who's the real star in this farce. No thanks, dear Alice, he said as he tossed the letter in the trash.

The Friday after the trial he had dinner with the Gilmores, in fact, two families of Gilmores, for Henry was also there with his wife Maggie. Kearney had known and liked them for many years, ever since his mother leased the water rights to Henry for his thirsty cattle. Naturally, however, he was more attached to

Harvey's family.

Congratulations to Kearney for the good verdict were the order of the day, but the centerpiece of the occasion was Dorothy's mouthwatering recipes. After long pleasant table conversation, Harvey invited Henry and Kearney to come with him to look at his new John Deere tractor.

"The old one was getting a little age on it, so I traded it in."

"Harvey, better watch that kind of talk," Henry admonished him. "These women will pick up on it and start thinking of trading us in for newer models."

"Daddy, you and Uncle Henry go on ahead," Becky said, ignoring the humor. "I want to borrow Kearney for a little bit to get his help with some artwork of mine."

Dorothy smiled across the dining room at Harvey and he grinned back at her. Becky and Kearney did not notice. Their relationship had budded to the point where their main interest was each other.

Title: *Louisiana Rogue*
- Author: Harold Raley
- Publisher: Lamar University Press
- Paper Back: ISBN: 9780985255275
- eBook: Kindle
- Pages 306
- Publication Date: April 2013

This wonderfully entertaining picaresque novel by Harold Raley falls in the tradition of rogue literature established by Tom Jones and other early novels. Set in the nineteenth century, Louisiana Rogue will take you on a wild, fast-paced romp through all levels of Cajun society in the 1830s. The title page says the book promises to tell "The Life and Times of Pierre Prospère-Tourmoulin, Picket-pocket, Thief, Gambler, Fugitive, Undertaker, Barber, Doctor, Priest, Prisoner, Bandit, and Count; Latterly penned in his hand for the gentle reader of leisure, Spanning the years 1831-1839" and claims to be translated by Peter Tourmoulin.

Title: *The Unknown God: Mysteries of Deity, Time, Space, and Creation*

- Author: Harold Raley
- Publisher: CreateSpace
- Paper Back: ISBN: 9781466273184
- Pages 142
- Publication Date: October, 2011

In his powerful Introduction to The Unknown God, religious thinker and writer Harold Raley makes this unusual request of the reader: "Suspend, if you will, everything you know about God. Put aside for the duration of this reading your traditional theologies and hear a new and more reverent way of thinking about God. When you return to your old understandings, they will have deeper meanings, unless those you once professed were meaningless to start with. If you are unwilling or unable to do as I ask, read no further. This message is not for you. The truth it contains will find you later when it is ready for you and you have been made ready for it." To approach Deity from this radically new perspective--arguably the greatest advance in theological thought of modern times--is to expose and shed light on the baffling paradoxes, improbable notions, and misleading errors not only about God but also about time, space, creation, and immortality. In each of these categories this book offers stunning new insights that incorporate not only the efforts of classical theologians but also the latest discoveries in science. Outline in these advanced insights is a new understanding of human life. By the law of corresponding identities, Raley explains, a more elevated theory of God necessarily means a more elevated theory of mankind. Each of the many themes and aperçus packed into this slender volume could have been a hefty tome. With pristine eloquence Raley reduces them to the essentials, believing as he does that clarity of style is courtesy to the reader.

Title: *The Light of Eden:*
A Christian Worldview
- Author: Harold Raley
- Publisher: John M. Hardy Publishing
- Paper Back: ISBN: 9780979839122
- Pages 196
- Publication Date: May 2008

An inspiring vision of richer Christian life and thought. In the tradition of C. S. Lewis and G. K. Chesterton, this extraordinary book is both a spiritual adventure and an intellectual feast. Packed with illuminating insights and written in beautiful language, The Light of Eden introduces its readers to a vast treasury of creative ideas, innovative concepts, and possibilities contained in Christianity.

Title: *The Spirit of Spain*
- Author: Harold Raley
- Publisher: Halcyon Pr Ltd
- Paper Back: ISBN: 9780970605498
- Pages 212
- Publication Date: October, 2011

The Spirit of Spain brims with aperçus and revelations, many of them controversial, others startling, all engrossing. From Roman Hispania to the most recent Spanish trends, Professor Raley narrates the unique story of Spanish civilization. Examples of his original thinking include a "phenomenology of Spanish history," a new theory of the Spanish Renaissance, new concepts of Spanish patriotism and nationalism, and a reinterpretation of Spanish "Stoicism." As the book unfolds he also takes many sidelong looks into Hispanic America and offers a new explanation of Spain's relationship to Moslem Al-Andalus and modern Europe. The book culminates in a radical analysis of "Quixotic life" and its unsuspected significance for the post-modern age.

Title: *The Prodigal*
- Author: Harold Raley
- Publisher: Mouse Gate Press
- Paper Back: ISBN: 9781590953402
- eBook ISBN: 9781590953419
- Pages 96
- Publication Date: October, 2016

In the tradition of Crusoe and Sabatini, The Prodigal is a story of the shipwreck and struggle for survival of a young ship's carpenter who escapes one captivity only to fall into more dangerous circumstances. The story unfolds from Boston to Mexico, Cuba, Africa, and back again. At critical points a mysterious stranger intervenes to lend a hand and guide him to his destiny.

Title: *Barefoot On A Frosty Morn*
- Author: Harold Raley
- Publisher: Mouse Gate Press
- Paper Back: ISBN: 9781590953426
- eBook ISBN: 9781590953433
- Pages 352
- Publication Date: October, 2016

Barefoot on a Frosty Morn is a literary and genealogical tapestry of several families over three centuries. The genealogical threads stretch back to England and France and unfold in step with America's continental expansion. The families crisscross north, south, and west as the tapestry grows in richness and complexity. A final episode sheds light on the earliest roots of the story. The reader has a perspective only partially available to the personalities immersed in the stories. Episodes are woven around some American milestones: the Revolution, the Civil War and WWII. These resonate and enrich but do not hinder the genealogical flow of the novel. In its conception and execution *Barefoot on a Frosty Morn* is unlike any writing before it. It surpasses the limits of history and narrates the essence of the American vision of life.

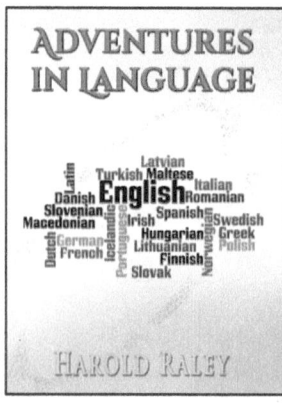

Title: *Adventures in Language*

- Author: Harold Raley
- Publisher: TotalRecall Publications
- Paper Back: ISBN: 9781590955321
- eBook ISBN: 9781590955352
- Pages 216
- Publication Date: October, 2017

In these *Adventures in Language* linguist Harold Raley explores fascinating features of English and many other languages in different cultures and historical eras.

Even though at times I point out obvious errors in the languages as they are currently structured, I realize that the rules of grammar and usage in English or any other living language are, or can be, subject to change. This may not be true of, say, ancient Sanskrit, but then we note that despite its perfection—or perhaps because of it—ancient Sanskrit ceased to be a spoken tongue many centuries ago.

Over the ages thinkers have pondered the qualities that define humanity and set mankind apart from other species. In my view, no stronger case than language can be made for human uniqueness. Animals can communicate and mimic but they cannot speak. Language, sung, recited, or spoken, is archly human, and for that reason also deeply mysterious, beautiful, and fascinating.

Title: *Points Of Light*

- Author: Harold Raley
- Publisher: TotalRecall Publications
- Paper Back: ISBN: 9781590955369
- eBook ISBN: 9781590955376
- Pages 238
- Publication Date: October, 2017

These *Points of Light* centered on the beauty, humor, and mystery of human life present many perspectives flowing out of the unifying philosophical premise that life, not physical reality, is the foundational reality in which all others are rooted.

A noted thinker once said that clarity is the courtesy an author extends to the reader. Insofar as my abilities permit, I have tried to add another kindness: word economy, which I understand to mean saying as much as possible in the fewest words. In those cases in which there is neither clarity nor economy, I alone take the blame.

Title: *Memories of Appalachia*
- Author: Harold Raley
- Publisher: TotalRecall Publications
- Paper Back: ISBN: 9781590956496
- eBook ISBN: 9781590956052
- Pages 296
- Publication Date: 2020

A celebrated philosopher once said that in order to understand anything human we must tell a story. However, this human narrative is not about what we are. That kind of information is the business of science, which teaches us about our physical nature. But the real story of our life, the human portion, is who we are, and it begins where science and nature end. Biography, not biology, is the true human narrative.

No one can write our narrative for us, and no one should. For we are the novelists of ourselves, the composers of our personal melody of life. Daily we add pages to our story or notes to our song. Animals, our only flesh and blood companions in this world, are what they are by Nature's decree, but we humans are who we become primarily by our personal choices. This means that of all God's creatures, only we have the freedom—and therefore the responsibility—to choose how we live our life, and if necessary, to reconsider, to rectify, to repent and rewrite our story if it is sordid or change our tune if our music is discordant.

I take these distinctions to heart in this writing. It is the story of the things I did for the first twenty years of my life and what happened to me as I did them. In a general sense, this is the description of any life, great or small, and mine conforms to the pattern with nothing exceptional to recommend it. Mine is the unremarkable tale of an obscure life in an obscure place. Yet I cannot dismiss it as insignificant, for that would imply that I am judge and jury of life's meaning, which I am not, not even of my own life, most of all, my own life.

Harold Raley

Title: *Tattletales*
- Author: Harold Raley
- Publisher: TotalRecall Publications
- Paper Back: ISBN: 9781648830044
- eBook ISBN: 9781648830051
- Pages 260
- Publication Date: 2020

A celebrated philosopher once said that in order to understand anything human we must tell a story. He spoke a profound truth, and it is important to understand some of its implications. Art, including musical and literary art, tells us very little about what we are. That kind of information is the business of science, which teaches that we are mammalian animals, first cousins to the great apes. On the other hand, art has much to tell us about who we are. It reminds us that we are persons, or better said, men and women, who daily add pages to a private narrative, or notes to an inimitable life melody. We are the novelists of ourselves. If we exist at a primary level as biological creatures subject to nature's laws and limitations, on a different plane we live as unique biographical persons whose mission is not to remain at nature's mercy but to humanize the world with artifact and artistry, creed and creativity, song and story. The thirteen tales in this book are modest examples of the high art of being human in a rich alchemy of styles, times, and climes.

Title: *Tides of Fortune*
- Author: Harold Raley
- Publisher: TotalRecall Publications
- Paper Back: ISBN: 9781648830068
- eBook ISBN: 9781648830075
- Pages 202
- Publication Date: 2020

These are tales of fortune and forfeiture, happiness and hazard, love and deceit. Some stories are set in specific times and places but not confined to them. Others arise in the mere vastness of the world and belong anywhere applicable or nowhere definitive. For wherever there is human life, there are the yearnings, dreams, possibilities and impossibilities we call tales and stories. For this reason, I do not think of myself as their creator, but only their author or perhaps their channeler. I say this because the people who come to life in this book do not always behave as I wish and plan. I push and they push back. Which is why I am as surprised as the next person by what they decide to do and who they choose to be. Perhaps their way is best. For if the decisions were left up to me, most likely I would be their tyrant. As it is, I end up being their friend.

www.ingramcontent.com/pod-product-compliance
Lightning Source LLC
Chambersburg PA
CBHW020633110726
47899CB00002B/761

*9 7 8 1 6 4 8 8 3 0 0 6 8 *